REDEEMED

Jeni Burns

Redeemed

Twisted Fate Novella #5

Copyright © 2016

Jeni Burns

c/o Jeni Burns

15105-D John J. Delaney Drive; #317

Charlotte, NC 28277

All rights reserved.

Cover Design By: Indira Jainanan

http://www.indirajartwork.com/

Print ISBNs
ISBN: 1-942964-12-9
ISBN-13: 978-1-942964-12-4

Acknowledgements:

With each book I worry I'll inevitably forget to thank someone, but once again, I'll do my best.

Thank you to my CRW, RWA, FF&P, and NJRW friends. You inspire me to no ends.

Thank you to my friends and family—the list being longer than my body. You all know who you are and how much I love you.

Thanks to Lara Stokes, Reagan Phillips, Denise Leton, Sophia Henry, and Melissa Shank for beta reading, critiquing, and believing in me. You ladies are my foundation. I always know you have my six and are only a few taps of my fingers away. I love you ladies!

Thanks to Indira Jainanan for another fabulous cover. Your talent continues to amaze me.

Thanks to everyone who helped edit including, but not limited to, Reagan Phillips, Denise Leton and Jan Carol. Without them, this book would be a punctuation and continuity nightmare.

A huge thank you shout out to the members of "Jeni's Little Devils." You are all so supportive and encouraging! I love getting to hear from you and hope this book is everything you hoped for. If it is, please thank Lara Stokes, Melissa Shank, and Reagan Phillips who told me my original ending wasn't good enough for Dema and Delila.

One last note of thanks to Jen Anderson, Vickie Rush, Brenda Onley, Jamie Pejo, and Tara

Goodfellow for being the best "super fans" a girl could ask for!! Love you all!!

With all my thanks,
~ j

To Lauriel Faltin & Reagan Phillips.

Without you wonderful women this book would still be without a proper name.

Thank you from the bottom of my heart!

ONE

DRAMMELECH

DRAMMELECH LURKED IN the afternoon shadows of the great oaks. They were as much a comfort as something could be to a monster like himself. His "Jersey Devil" title undeniable in his current form; wings and tail unable to hide beneath the convention of clothing. He remembered his father wearing a cloak in the old days to conceal what exposed his otherness, but why hide his power? Why cower before the humans?

Distaste coated his split tongue like a bitter film. *Humans.* Not good for anything. Although, their endless willingness to barter their souls gave him something to do while he waited.

Daphne.

A voice in the back of his mind begged him to fly off to search for the missing key; the key that would grant him rule over the Overworld, Underworld, and this abomination humans called 'Earth.'

But the couple tangled in the front seat of the car parked on the otherwise deserted road piqued his interest much more. He cocked his head to the side and considered what they would be willing to sacrifice to save their lives. Hmm. Maybe he'd only offer a deal to one of them.

A rare smile slipped across his face and the feathers on his wings prickled to attention. Before he could contain it, laughter erupted from deep within his chest and alerted the amorous couple to his presence.

There were worse ways to make an entrance.

"Oh-my-God," gushed the red-haired woman as she pointed at him, lipstick smeared across her face.

"Silly girl. I'm the farthest thing from your God." It'd been a long time since he'd had this kind of fun for the sake of pure entertainment.

"Dude. Get outta here. Can't you see we're busy?"

Drammelech considered the man pinned to the seat beneath the woman's thighs. The human seemed unconcerned by both his nakedness and demon appearance.

"Oh, I sssssssee you." He raised an eyebrow. "But you've seen me. There's not much I can do to ssssave you now."

The woman froze. Terror lit her eyes and the corners sparkled with the threat of tears. Her lover swore and attempted to lift her off his lap. The steering wheel pinned her in place under Drammelech's quiet command.

"Who wants to die today?" His benign nonchalance contradicted the malevolent question. "I only need one more soul to make my quota this month, and any extra would be seen as showing off at my 'Devils Anonymous' meeting."

The silence in the woods surrounding the Merrill Creek Reservoir was perfect for this. In the distance, water drummed against a graveyard of dead trees in time with the hum of mosquitos not far from where he stood. He studied the people and weighed his options. The woman would spark a greater sense of urgency in his targets. Although, from the bundle of exposed muscle in the man's arms, maybe he'd be a better tool. He stepped closer to the vehicle.

"Take him," the woman cried. "I'm not ready to die." A hiccup erupted and her voice broke.

"What the fuck, Christine?"

"I can't die. I'm too young. I have too much life left in me." Her words dissolved into hysterics.

"Looks like you've made it easy for me." Drammelech spread his wings to their full breadth. His tail flicked back and forth. His forked tongue

9

savored the flavor of their fear in the air. Each purposeful pace forward was perfection.

Such a simple thing.

Stalk. Enslave. Kill. Rinse. Repeat.

His future never looked brighter.

The woman slammed the lock mechanism in place and her face paled behind the closing window glass. It was a shame he'd stain the vintage car. With a flick of his wrist, the lock popped up and the handle released in his grip. The door swung outward and the woman screamed. Her high-pitched shriek solidified his decision.

He wrapped a hand in her long locks and pulled. His wings beat behind him, stirring up a fanfare of fallen leaves.

Her nails dug into the man's chest, red dotted trails of blood followed in their retreating wake. Copper tickled his nose and every nerve ending in his devilish body sparked to life ready for the hunt.

One last hard yank and she fell from the car in a heap. He dropped her mane and tipped her chin toward his eyes. "You have a ten-second head start."

She sat still, transfixed.

It was a common reaction. One a former lover had dubbed 'devil desire'. She'd claimed it was impossible not to get lost in his dark chocolate colored eyes and sharp features. Then she'd sink to her knees and give him whatever he demanded. Including the child who paved the road of his life's journey.

Daphne.

He shook Daphne from his mind and concentrated on the memory of Cecily Barren instead. Cecily had given him many gifts. Sweet treats. Secret glances. Seductive moans. All with the scent of cocoa chasing her in a cloud. Staring at the whimpering woman on the ground, he shuddered. If all women were like Cecily had been, maybe he'd have more use for them.

He removed his finger from her pale skin. "Run."

He stepped back and waited for her to scramble to her feet. They always did. They always believed they stood a chance against him. He smirked as she turned and darted barefoot into the trees surrounding the narrow road.

Drammelech turned eyes back to the man still anchored in the seat. His shirt laid on the floorboards and his pants were twisted around his ankles.

"Don't worry. I'll make it painful." He winked.

At his words the man shook and whatever bravado he'd been conjuring crumbled. Tears broke free from their prison and streamed down his face.

Drammelech removed the key from the ignition, tossed it toward the water in the distance, and slammed the door.

"Don't move a muscle," he warned, then took off into the trees. He caught a whiff of the woman's fear to the left and darted after it. He needed a release—and not the kind the couple had been chasing. *No*. He needed to bathe in the blood of a human. To quench a thirst no beverage touched.

11

Ragged breaths vibrated in the air to his immediate right. He paused, the chase over. Sobs shook her heaving chest when he stepped into view.

Ahh.

Relief surged through him. Images of her slain body danced behind his eyes. So many possible ways to die, so little time.

He reached his hand across the small distance between them. Skin so soft. Fragile. *Human.*

She stepped toward him, resignation and bargaining in her stance. "Please."

The soft plea did little to sway him. He nodded a silent commitment he had no intention of keeping, then pulled her into his arms. She shivered in his embrace, the friction of their nakedness sparking something dormant deep inside him.

Drammelech's wings flared and together they rose into the sky. High above the trees he trailed a line of kisses from beneath her ear to the sweat-slicked hollow of her throat. Unsaid promises made her pliant in his grasp. She turned a set of confused emerald eyes on him and laid her lips on his.

He waited a beat until her lashes fluttered closed. *They always closed their eyes.* As if viewing the devil's face as they succumbed was too much to process. When her crimson lashes brushed her ivory skin, he released her into nothingness.

He hovered as her eyes shot wide, limbs flailed against the crisp air, and realization sunk in. Branches grabbed at her perfect skin, tore into it like talons. Snapping branches and bones cracked—music to his ears. A crescendo of cries anchored him to the moment. Unable to achieve the contentment he craved at this altitude, he dove through the colored leaf canopy.

Her body grappled for purchase, graceful, gorgeous—he was close. Her body arched in a last attempt to defy gravity before it hit the ground. His release took hold as a moan escaped her quivering lips, the air rushing from her in a broken splintered gush.

Ahh.

He could breathe again. Concentrate. Focus.

Daphne.

Not again.

Not so soon.

If he didn't have Daphne in his possession soon, he wasn't sure he could keep the rest of humanity alive long enough to rule them.

The sound of a car door opening called to him. He had another victim waiting. He didn't need a pawn to get what he wanted. He needed to focus. To concentrate. To think. *Just one more release*, he promised himself. *One more.*

Drammelech snaked through the sky toward the vintage car. This time, there'd be blood.

Two

Daphne

DAPHNE BARREN DIDN'T want to die, but with being the prophesied key to the Overworld, and the Jersey Devil having her in his sights, options were a luxury she didn't have. The thought repeated like a cassette tape single stuck in the player of an old car. She didn't want to die. Not today. Not tomorrow. Not before seeing her family one last time. Not before at least reclaiming her body from the witch whose spirit currently rebuffed her every attempt to take control back. Not before seeing if Colin DeGrasse was as solid beneath his clothes as she imagined.

Heat flared to life across her face despite Delila's control. *What was she thinking*? Better yet, who did the thought belong to? She glanced at the man in question from the corner of her eye and studied him as he navigated her brother, Nic's SUV toward the Dewsberry land in Harmony.

Without her imprisoned front row seat to view him through, surely she'd be a drooling idiot of a mess right there, riding shotgun. The possibility of this as an upside to being locked inside her body crossed her mind. She tried to shake the thought away, but it refused. Her thoughts were all she had. Even those she didn't entirely trust because somewhere, bouncing around in her head, screamed the notion that she couldn't wait to hop in bed with the devil. Not the devil who wanted her dead, but the mack daddy of all devils. The ruler of the Underworld. The torturer of souls slated for eternal damnation. And shit if she wasn't a little aroused by the thought. Or could it be that the hunk of a man to her left sent her senses into overdrive despite his body being the devil's current vessel?

Another glance at Colin settled her internal debate. Sleeping with one devil to avoid being murdered by another was most definitely the way to go. Her hand reached across the empty space between her body and Colin's and landed with purpose on his thigh. Embarrassment ripped through the bits of her she could access, but those weren't the ones responsible for removing her hand. Nope. It stayed firmly planted on his thigh and moved its way toward his crotch.

She wanted to scream. To tell Delila to stop. To beg Colin to realize this wasn't her. She wouldn't ever be so daring. Especially under these circumstances--on the run, with her best friend tied up in the backseat, kidnapped, for all intents from the devil who wanted them all dead. Not to mention being possessed by the mother of all witches and the King of Hell waiting for them. *Ugh*.

Being trapped in her body reeked of torture; like old mind control films back in the Cold War era. Eyes trained on something she didn't want to see, ears unable to ignore the messages coming at her. Her body pinned in place, exposed to someone else's mercy. She, a shackled prisoner, the warden planned to use for things she dared not think about.

The lust in Colin's eyes won 'most untimely' realization of the day. Whether it belonged to the devil Delila called Dema or Colin, she didn't know. But there was no mistaking it. The sweet, cautious, protective gaze of Colin's had been replaced with one dripping with longing, desire, and hunger. She earned the title of 'prey', thanks to Delila. The bitch had no problems overstepping boundaries. Not even a little. No evidence needed beyond the growing bulge beneath Colin's jeans to explain his thoughts on the matter.

Not including her two brothers, she's managed to go almost twenty-six years without seeing a man's junk. Today, all those years of innocence would go down in a blaze of hellfire. Because, of course, the first man she'd sleep with would be possessed by the devil. If she could scream and claw her way to the surface she would, but Delila wouldn't have it. She was a powerful witch. Too powerful. Even as a damn spirit.

Not the devil, Colin, chimed in the part of her brain she still controlled. She needed to believe that. Keep it all in perspective. There were worse guys to lose her virginity to. Strong, sweet Colin had a protective streak broader than his sexy shoulders. She could do worse for her first time. Her hand caressed him through his jeans at Delila's command and Daphne melted under the flash of heat. If she died from embarrassment, maybe the inevitable wouldn't count.

A moan stuck in his throat and he reached across the space between them and pressed the heel of his hand into the apex of her jeans.

"I've waited far too long," the devil mused in Colin's voice.

THREE

DELILA

DELILA'S HOST FOUGHT for control. She sent the equivalent of a mental shove back at Daphne's essence. Delila was stronger and she relished knowing that until she was ready to let Daphne have full control, the body she wore was hers to use as she wanted.

Inhabiting her descendant had seemed like a good idea at the time. How often did a willing body come along and invite a spirit in? In her over three hundred years as an incorporeal being, she knew the numbers were low on welcoming hosts. At first, Daphne allowed her full control over the body, but now as they neared her family farm, the struggle between them bubbled over into a full-fledged fight, as if they both were trying to squeeze into the same formfitting dress.

Sure, she could waft into the background and let Daphne take the reins, but where was the fun in that? Besides, Daphne and the male witch had come to her for help. And now that Dema was on board, she had nothing to lose. If anyone would be able to put their son in his rightful place, it was Dema.

The anxious anticipation of his arrival still hadn't worn off, she realized as another jolt of adrenaline arched through her bloodstream. Surely, the chemicals coursing through her weren't all because of some leftover affections for him, were they? She flexed the hand on his crotch and peeked at him from under the protection of Daphne's lashes. He shifted closer in his seat and grinned in response to her caress, his hand flexing against her. Despite the silver eyes and closely cropped locks, she could imagine Dema beneath the skin of this man and it drove her crazy. She brushed lazy fingers over the growing protrusion in his jeans and sighed.

Too many years had passed since she'd last laid hands on the man who'd always been close to her heart. She would've given anything to change the outcome of their love affair, but she'd been young and naive. It didn't help that their son had conspired to tear them apart hundreds of years ago. Until today, they'd been unable to hash out the troubles between them. Based on the swell beneath her fingertips, it seemed all was forgiven. Or soon to be.

"I've missed you, darling." Her words sounded strained with Daphne's voice. The woman was fighting again.

"De-li-la."

Even with the other man's voice toying with the drawn out syllables, she could hear Dema's voice

19

as if he was in his corporal form and not this human-hijacked version.

"It's been too long."

"You are as familiar to me today, in that body, as if no time at all has passed." He clasped her hand in his lap and held it tight. "If I didn't have the years of longing still fresh in my memory, my witch, I'd believe it was only yesterday when I held you last."

A jolt of electricity coursed through her body at his soft words. "Does that mean you've forgiven me?" She leaned away from the hulking stature of her returned lover and watched for any indication of a grudge.

The smile on his face never wavered.

"Are you two done?" The male witch in the backseat cut in. "She's resorted to biting and if we don't get to the farm soon, I'm going to have to spell her."

How had she so easily forgotten the witches in the backseat? Having Dema beside her after so many years stood front and center to everything right now. She closed her eyes and let the memories assault her. Sun-kissed summers, sweat-slicked bodies, flying, soaring, release. A shiver raced up her spine and Daphne shrank back into the depths of their shared body. Her host was embarrassed? *Interesting*. The man sitting beside them was a perfect male specimen and she was certain Daphne agreed.

Jason thrust his head between the front seats. "Seriously, guys. Can you drop Callie and I at the house? I'll see if Gramps can get through to her."

"Sure."

Dema's one-word answer said more than a thousand words could. But it was his searing stare that sent shockwaves straight to her core.

Four

Daphne

Callie's screams in the backseat were matched with Jason's curses and mumbled spells. At least Daphne hoped he was spelling her best friend into submission. If it were up to her to save Callie, they both would be sunk. Delila was hell bent on enjoying her reunion with Dema and Daphne was along for the ride whether she wanted to be or not. Between the heated looks Dema sent her way, she could almost imagine Colin apologizing.

Her new friend wouldn't let this happen if he had a choice. She believed it with her whole heart. He was the guy who came to her rescue—and she was an unknown stranger. A man like that would never take advantage of a woman. And yet, here they found themselves. At a crossroad. The intersection of reunited-lover-body-snatcher's sex and strangers fumbling in the dark on Morningwood Ave.

"Let me out of this damn car. Elech will kill us all. You know taking me didn't save anyone, you stupid jerk. All you did was piss him off."

Callie's cries bounced around the car and collided with Daphne's sense of self-preservation.

"Look. Jason did what he thought was best. Give it a rest." The words were hers! She'd thought them and they'd come from her mouth without Delila interfering. Maybe there was a chance she could reclaim her body after all.

The car dipped as Colin/Dema turned down the gravel driveway of the Dewsberry farmlands and bounced along the rutted drive until the house came into sight.

"It looks like time stood still."

Hearing Dema's words in Colin's voice was creepy. He pulled the car to a stop and Jason dragged Callie from the backseat.

"I know the two of you want some alone time, but you've got an hour until I come looking for you and I don't want to see more than I should. Got it?" Jason's scolding tone sent a flame of heat to her cheeks. Did everyone know what was about to happen? Seriously?

Daphne gave Colin a quick glance out of the side of her eyes and sized him up. Sure, he was handsome. He was kind and thoughtful. But he was huge. His arms were thick with corded muscle, his shoulders strong enough to lift tree trunks out of the way. Probably from any time spent in the other forms she'd seen him shift into when Jason

23

had gotten some of the *Reveal* potion on him when they confronted Elech last.

She wasn't sure exactly what Colin was that made him more "other" than human, but witnessing his transition from animal to animal had been a beautiful sight. One she'd remember forever. And if they ever found themselves free from this body snatcher hell, she'd ask him to show her again. Slowly this time, so she could try to guess which was his most true form.

"Where to?"

His deep voice was smooth, like fine silk or decadent chocolate and it sank within her and melted her to the core. Was the reaction hers or Delila's? She tried to speak, but nothing came out. Guess her fleeting control had fled.

"The barn." Her voice, Delila's words.

"So many fond memories there." His words sent a shiver down their combined spine.

Good gravy. She needed to get a grip. And not of Colin. Or Dema. Or whoever he was. If there was even a hope of taking back her body, her life, her fucking future, she needed a plan. One that would make her death painless when the showdown with the devil took place. Because it was inevitable. Much as she wished otherwise, she knew it was true. She was going to die by his hands or be forced to work by his side. And current circumstances notwithstanding, she wasn't about to spend her life as a devil's pet.

The barn came into full view as Colin wrapped his arm around her waist, tugging her closer to him in the front seat.

"It's just you and me now." He eased the car to a stop and shifted in to park. "Let's see if we can remember where we left off." He tugged her over the center console and out his door behind him.

Dread sank through her as her puppet master wrapped her arms around Colin's waist and her own voice chimed in with, "I think last time you weren't wearing any clothes."

There was nothing like knowing you were about to lose your virginity to the devil.

A low chuckle broke through her thoughts as they stepped over the threshold into the barn. He led her to an empty stall. One that opened to the rear of the property with a huge split door. A horse stall perhaps.

"Ahh, if I remember correctly," Dema reminisced as he tugged at Colin's belt. "Neither were you."

Oh shit.

⋆⋆⋆⋆⋆

Wow. Everything about Colin was impressive. From the breadth of his shoulders, to his ability to shift, and downright to the size of his… *Damn.* There was no way Daphne should be thinking like this. Not when her existence was being threatened. But, hot damn. How come she couldn't have met him under any other circumstances? One where they bumped into each other in the Dews perhaps, or at the hardware store. Hell, why couldn't he have been the guy who placed a missed connections ad in the paper only days ago? Had she even thought a guy like Colin could be behind such an ad, she wouldn't've fought Callie so much on responding. Any of those options would be better than, "I think we've both had our bodies taken by dead and demonic star-crossed lovers who created the biggest bad guy in the history of bad guys."

Yeah, Colin was hunky in a drool-worthy, I-will-save-you kind of way. Until his shape began to shift; the solid lines of his shape blurring into hard to see ridges and valleys. Then he doubled over and howled as his shirt ripped into shreds around him and wings, huge, black feathered wings, erupted from between his shoulder blades. Soon, everything that screamed Colin was replaced by what she could only assume was Dema. Except for the blazing silver of his eyes.

Dema wafted through her thoughts on a whim like a dandelion floret on a warm summer breeze. Delila controlled her too easily. There was no doubt of who was in charge of their shared body.

Especially since her clothes were falling to the floor in quick order as her body bared itself to Colin, no, Dema. *Oh crap*. This was about to get confusing.

"I don't want you to mistake who will bring you pleasure, my love."

"Dema." The sigh of his name made her shiver. Damn Delila's love for this demon. "I would never mistake him for you." Delila's words hung heavy in the pheromone-full air between them. "I wish I could offer you *my* body, though."

"Darling, we will find a way to be together again. Until then, this body will do nicely. Although, I do prefer your golden locks to these." He reached a hand out and tucked a dark strand of hair behind her ear.

Daphne willed her eyes to close as Dema's lips brushed hers. Imagining Colin on the other side of her eyelids was the only way she'd get through this without losing her mind. And it was Colin's face that exploded in her mind behind her closed lids. A tantalizing image of his stunning silver eyes locked on her as a thin gold band wove its way around them, anchoring them to one another. Her heart raced. Never had a kiss felt so... permanent.

Without hesitation, her hands brushed against the solid muscle of his chest, the warmth of it tantalizing. They paused long enough for the brush of heat between them to ratchet up a notch, before they slipped lower, lower, and lower still. Oh. Oh. Oh. Whether it be Dema or Colin, she didn't dare allow Delila to open her eyes, but the hefty weight of his erection in her hand made her mouth go dry. This was happening. She was about to screw the devil.

No.

Colin.

She was going to have sex with Colin.

27

Yeah.

Colin.

Caring. Collected. Colin.

All thoughts ceased as his fingers parted her folds and he strummed the bundle of nerves at their apex. His tongue slipped past her lips and probed her mouth as his fingers probed a much more tender spot. *Goodness gracious.*

Her legs buckled beneath her. Bones failed to hold her.

"I've been dreaming of your legs wrapped around me for decades," he whispered as he hoisted her against him.

A well-placed hand on her backside braced her against him as he rubbed himself against her entrance. Something swirled around her ankle, snakelike and slithery. She kicked at the offending item, shaking off the sinking sensation of being gobbled up whole by a snake. Her fight and flight instincts sparked to life with a shot.

"Darling, you never minded my tail before," the devil whispered as he found her entrance and thrust as deep as her body allowed.

A small whimper erupted from her mouth, unbidden, as a quick shot of pain lanced through her. This was it. She was officially having sex for the first time. With the devil. *No. With Colin.*

The tail snaked its way up her long leg. *No.* She shuddered. She couldn't do this. Not even with the smell of Colin's sandalwood scent in her nostrils could she convince herself the man she'd spent time ogling and daydreaming about was the same as the beast with the tail.

Retreating to a shadowy place in her mind, she forbade herself to accept the notion of losing her virginity to Dema. She let Delila take control. Gave her everything. Every touch. Every sound. Every breath.

When she finally detached herself from the physical sensations of her body, everything inside shattered into a million embers of sparkling light. She, herself, was only held together by a thin strand of gold twine in her mind's eye as the pounding of Colin's heart mirrored her own. As the overwhelming sensations receded, her voice echoed in the quiet of her mind. She reached for the feel of Delila and found the space she'd occupied only minutes ago, empty.

"Daphne."

The low pitch of Colin's voice called every nerve ending to attention. Wrapped in his strong arms, she embraced what made him all male deep inside her flesh. She dared open an eye and was relieved to find his familiar face lost in the heat of the moment before her. His form vibrated between his human one and the frame of Dema's natural appearance. With the steadfast vision of Colin in her mind, the friction inside eased from discomfort to pleasure. She refused to think this through; refused to question how it came to be that Dema and Delila were gone and Colin and she were free. She needed to get a grip. A grip on what she wasn't sure, so she secured her arms around Colin's neck and begged her brain to believe this joining was kismet or at the very least, the universe's way of giving her a much-needed break.

The feel of Colin's hands on her skin shook away the errant thoughts. She succumbed to his touch without a hint of regret.

Anticipation built like a thunderstorm in the distance and rolled over her with the force of an oncoming wave. Here she was, perched on a virtual stranger's waist, falling into the bliss of orgasm as her back raked against the cool wooden wall of a horse stall—and she never felt more alive in her life. She moaned and rode the wave, unable to care about who or what had gotten her to this place, only glad she was there.

Oh. My. Goddess. Overwhelming took on a new meaning when Daphne found herself scrambling to the surface within her own body, no longer a bystander, to what was going on around, or, in her. The swell of Colin's cock deep inside of her registered as the only solid bit of sanity she could wrap her brain around. A smack on her ass stung as she came fully aware of herself and able to control her body. Too bad her traitorous body screamed with pleasure rather than push away from the beast holding her. And beast was the best description she could make. Colin's face took on the long angular slopes. His hyper aware silver eyes were stunning. Breathtaking even. The soft velvety feel of his strong wings holding her tight warred with the hard bands of his arms wound around her, refusing to let even a hint of cool air come between their superheated bodies. And that naughty tail. *Good gracious.* It had a mind of its own and it was challenging even her most adventurous sensibilities. His relentless hips, exploring tail, and nimble lips, had her cresting another hill of pleasure before she could catch her breath.

She was so close... So close to reaching the peak... So close to screaming out Colin's name. And then the beast holding her moaned 'Daphne' in her ear. He demanded her release. Stern, soft, a summons all the same. And before she could hold back, the dam broke free and opened to him, giving him all he wanted, no, needed, no, *claimed* for his own.

She was his. Dema's. No. Colin's.

It was indisputable. Undeniable. *Fuck.* She wanted to do it again. But before she could beg for him or, hell, whimper in her bliss, his release followed hers, pulsing, heated, heavenly. If the words, 'Good God' left her lips, she wasn't sure, but they surely floated through her brain.

From somewhere near, she heard her name. Who in their right mind would be calling her at a time like this?

Oh shit. Her eyes flew open and were met with the glowing silver of Colin's eyes set deep in his ruggedly handsome face and not the angular planes his face had taken on under Dema's influence. His face was taunt and he held her tight as his release stole his breath. She no longer was

31

wrapped in a winged embrace, but safely tucked in Colin's steel-banded arms.

"Colin?" The question was a whisper, one she almost instantly wanted to draw back when acknowledgment flashed across his face.

"Oh, shit." He froze as if panic whipped through him. He slid from her body and released his strong grip. "Daphne?"

She stumbled to right herself, and landed flush against him even more so than she'd been only moments ago in their intimacy. His still-damp cock pressed against her stomach and twitched.

"In the flesh?" She aimed for funny, but landed on meek and insecure while a piece of her died of embarrassment.

"Oh God, Daphne. I'm so sorry. I don't know what happened. I…"

She stepped back and immediately regretted her decision as the cool air between them brought her nipples to stiff peaks. Unsure what to cover first, she bowed her head and hoped her hair would cover at least something, only it gave her a fully-aware, couldn't-blame-it-on-her-body-snatcher view of Colin's maleness. *All* of it. She swallowed and closed her eyes as heat rushed to her cheeks in a flaming proclamation.

"It's not your fault. I think our…" she struggled to find the right word to describe Delila and Dema, "guests?" Close enough. "I think they needed to get something off their chests." She spun her back on him and opened her eyes, frantic to find her clothes. By the stall door, a pile of garments glowed like a beacon of hope. If she could just get dressed this would be easier to deal with. Standing naked in a barn with someone who was a complete stranger not so long ago, with his seed running down the inside of her thigh was not her best moment. Not by a long shot.

She rushed to the clothes and the first item her fingers touched was denim. Not hers, his. She reached for the jeans, intending to toss it behind her to the silent man, but a whiff of his scent tickled her nose and made her pause. The mix of maleness and sandalwood would forever be linked to him, to right now, to this time in her life when she'd been free. *Free?* Where had that thought come from? She held the jeans to her bare chest and took a beat to compose herself.

"I think it's best if we don't talk about this." Her voice shook and her hands followed.

His low voice rumbled over her skin, as he approached, setting her nerves ablaze once more. "Are you sure? I mean, I thought women liked to talk things over. Especially things like this. Because if I'd had a say in this, we'd at least gone on a few dates first." A hand reached out and swept her hair off her back, gently settling it over her shoulder. A tender kiss at the pulse-point beneath her ear had her ready to swoon, throw her arms around him, and beg him to take her again. This time, both of them in control. She shook the thought away and grabbed the next item from the pile at her feet. Her shirt. *Score!* She whirled on Colin, thrust his jeans into his chiseled chest without waiting for him to grasp the denim and slid her shirt over her exposed breasts.

"Someone's outside and I don't want them seeing," she trailed off as her blush heated her cheeks again. "I don't want them to know what happened." She scooped up her jeans and her underwear fell from the waistband. "Shit."

"Allow me."

Colin reached for the black lace and satin thong at the same time she did. Her fingers fell away and she moved out of his orbit, lest she get sucked into him again. She tugged her jeans on, one leg at a time and hopped into them. "Keep 'em." She called as she stuffed her feet into her shoes and ran for the door.

There was no graceful exit after a romp in the barn. At least, not for her.

Five

Daphne

"Daphne? Are you in there?" Jason's voice echoed in the empty barn, bouncing off all the wooden surfaces.

Daphne could feel the heat of her blush renew with vigor. She burst from the horse stall and hoped Jason wouldn't notice. She stopped short and studied the man's face. "What's wrong? Where's Callie?"

The sound of chanting reached her ears and dread settled in her stomach.

"She's outside. Not even Gramps could get through to her. She pulled a knife and threatened to kill him."

"What? No! She would never do that. Not to Gramps." Nerve endings she didn't know she had sparked to life, aware of Colin's nearness in the doorway behind her.

"Is everything okay?" The deep rumble of Colin's voice sent a shiver down her spine.

"Yeah. I tried to magically sedate her," Jason replied. "It didn't last long, but gave me time to get her hands bound." He scrubbed a hand across his face. "I'm not sure what to do with her."

The defeat in his words broke her heart. She would do anything for this man. He'd already done so much for her all because he felt he owed a debt to her best friend. She pushed past him into the crisp fall air and made a beeline for Callie.

"I'm not sure what's gotten in to you, but this has got to stop." She poked a finger into her best friend's chest and glared. "I mean it. Jason saved you from Elech. Not harmed you. Not kidnapped you. Saved you. So, how about shutting your trap and showing a little gratitude?" All the emotions she'd been forcing into the back of her mind erupted in one big ball of fury. She stooped down to meet Callie's eyes where she knelt on the ground. "This is not your fight. This is mine. So, buck up and shake off whatever Elech did to you. I need your help if there's any chance of saving any of us. I can't do it alone. I need you." Without waiting for a response, she threw her arms around Callie and cried.

They'd been through so much together. All the loss they carried with them was equally shared across their shoulders. When one fell, the other picked them up. When one needed to dance, the other sang. They were more than friends, they were family. The kind of family not given to them at birth, but the kind forged in the fires of Hell and tested by life, time and time again. There was no way she would let Callie be enslaved by the devil any longer. She gathered every ounce of courage she possessed, released her friend, and stood to her full height. The fine hairs on her arms rose as her subconscious became aware of Colin and Jason behind her.

"I'll turn myself over to Elech. It's the only way to make this end." Her proclamation was the ending of a story that had been going on for far too long. She'd known her destiny for years and it was time she finally embraced it. She'd turn herself over to Elech and barter for the safety of everyone she cared for. Then, before he could make her open the gates to the Overworld, she'd kill herself. It would be the only way to ensure his torment ended.

"No." Jason yelled and pointed a finger toward a wilted and crying Callie. "I promised her I would keep you safe." He swiveled toward Colin and pointed at him. "He swore to help me keep *you* safe. Do you really think we'd let you declare you've quit and just shrug our shoulders and say, 'okay?'" He shot her with a glare. "Did you really think we'd give up? So Delila and Dema weren't as helpful as we had hoped. And losing Dax was unfortunate, but they aren't reasons to quit."

"Grams is dead. My mom has been in a soul-less coma for almost thirteen years. My brother is dead." Her voice rose and her body shook, but she continued. "My best friend is under the devil's compulsion. And I just had sex for the first time with the devil in his body," she whirled on Colin, index finger outstretched. "What else is there for us? More death? More loss? I don't want to be the reason the world as we know it ends and that's exactly what will happen if I open the gates for Elech. So, I won't. I'll fight him. I'll lose. And you'll all be safe." Tears streamed down her face and she ached with the pain of her honesty.

Strong arms wound around her and hugged her close. "I'm so sorry, Daphne. I didn't know." He pulled her tight against his shirtless body and whispered in her ear. "I'll do anything to fix this for you. Let me help you. I can let Dema back in. I'm sure he's powerful enough to take Elech down." Colin brushed a soft kiss on her temple. "Don't give up. I'll fix this. It's the least I can do after what happened in the barn. I should've fought him harder…" His voice trailed off into nothingness.

"I don't blame you for any of this. You were trying to help." She wiggled out of his embrace and turned to Jason. "I need you to help me figure out how to contact Elech."

"We need more of a plan than that, Daphne."

"I can contact him," Callie's voice was clear for the first time since they'd taken her from Elech's side. "I can still feel his hold, but it seems to be weakening." She turned to Jason and asked, "Can we take the ropes off? I promise if I feel my control slipping, I'll help you put them back on."

Daphne didn't wait for Jason to answer. She ran to her friend and began working at the knot binding her hands together. "Welcome back. I knew he couldn't control you forever."

"I'm not sure he doesn't still have a hold on me though," Callie cautioned. "Are you sure you want to take this risk?"

"I've had my ancestor's ghost take over my body and mate with her long lost devilish lover. I think untying you is a risk I'm willing to take." A smile crept across her lips as her fingers loosened the rope enough that Callie could slip her hands out. The hug Callie wrapped her in was a welcome surprise.

"Whatever it takes, we'll get this all sorted out. I promise."

A cloud of dust wafted up farther down the drive. "Who's that?" She mused aloud as the car stopped by the main house.

"Probably Nic. I asked Gramps to call him," Jason answered as he inched closer to Callie.

"He should stay as far away from this as he can. After what Elech did to Dax, I don't want him getting involved." Panic coursed through her body with renewed vigor. "Send him away." Her voice dropped, "Please? I can't let him get himself killed, too. I can't lose anyone else."

"Not sure there's anything that would stop him from helping anyway. Knowing your brother, stubborn should've been his middle name." Callie soothed her with a gentle squeeze. "Let him help. He lost so much already. I'm sure he wants to do whatever he can to keep from losing you, too."

She nodded and closed her eyes against the fear coursing through her body at warp speed. This was it. Her army against the Jersey Devil was all here and accounted for. Each well aware death may wait for them at the end of this journey. All braced for the worst, but hopeful for the best. Brave. Steadfast. Loyal.

This was the meaning of life. Her true purpose. To stand against evil and fight beside the strongest people she knew with the hope that they could claim victory in the end. Now, all she needed was the strength to believe it.

Six

Drammelech

THE ALLURE OF destroying the mouthy blond woman was almost more than Elech could contain. He recognized her from the other night.

Daphne.

He shook the name from his head and concentrated on the woman before him. She was huddled in the corner of the hospital waiting room, her skin the color of pea soup. He'd already witnessed her retching in a nearby trashcan as she waited for a nurse to call her name.

It struck him odd that she didn't look upset. Considering she had witnessed him killing her supposed beloved, she paid him not even a second glance. Her eyes didn't hold the tell-tale ring of red reserved for the grieving. Instead, she clutched her stomach and shuddered.

A tall man strode through the door, an air of authority in his wake as he went right to her side. Elech cocked his head to the side and wrapped his jacket tighter around his body.

"Maureen? What's wrong?"

"Charlie," she sobbed. "I didn't know who else to call."

Recognition washed over Elech. The man had been at Daphne's after he'd killed her grandmother. And at the woman's house after he'd killed Dax.

Daphne.

Damn it. A snarl escaped unencumbered. Before he could consider his collapsing confidence, the thin hold on Callie snapped. There one minute. Gone the next.

Daphne.

Elech rose to his feet and brushed past the man now holding Maureen's hand. Her death would have to wait. He had a date with destiny.

Daphne.

SEVEN

DELILA

INCORPOREAL WAS NOT the state Delila preferred. Not even a little bit. First, things wafted through her. Second, she wafted through things. And third, a corporeal body was something she missed more than kissing her kids at night. It hadn't been until she'd had her all-too-brief time in Daphne's body that she realized how much she missed being human. Anger welled up in the core of her soul and threatened to spill out into the space around her, but in her current state none of the humans milling around the grounds of her home would even notice.

Delila wanted to slam her fist against the barn wall, something to announce herself, but it was no use. She was tired. As much as her tryst with Dema had reawakened a part of her she had thought long gone, it had used the last of her energy. She glanced around the barn hoping to find evidence of her lover somewhere. She'd been expelled from Daphne's body unexpectedly and the same had happened to Dema. She'd witnessed his expulsion, but he seemed nowhere to be found.

Her magic must've been rusty when she'd conjured him since only his essence had come through from the Underworld and not his full self as he had when she'd walked the Earth in her goddess-given body. Something unseen tugged at her and lured her away from the scene playing out amongst her human descendants inside her old horse barn. She pushed her ghostly presence through the wall of the barn out into the old pasture, overgrown from disuse. Sadness crept into her emotional palate and took root. In the distance, where fields should be, roof peaks stood tall. Nothing ever stayed the same. Not after so much time passed.

She stopped at the graveyard where her kin were buried. Everyone she had ever loved, besides Dema, rested here. And one day soon, she would too, so long as the people back at the barn saw fit to lay her now exposed bones to rest. An errant thought slipped through all the others. Would burying her bones be the end of her? The end of this existence she'd both cherished and hated for more years than she could remember?

The place in her chest where a mortal heart would be, fractured into a thousand and three tiny little pieces of regret. A warm hand landed on her shoulder and pulled her back.

Dema.

She'd know the weight of his hand anywhere. This time he was as solid as the rest of the humans walking this plane.

"How is it you have a body now?"

"After our amorous interlude, I was expelled from the Elemental's body and returned here." He slid his finger under where her chin should be. "I found the door to the Underworld ajar and was able to pass through again in my full form. I assumed it was thanks to your forgiveness and trust."

She lowered her gaze and studied the silken rope that secured his robe. It was hard to see him in the flesh and know she had nothing more to offer him.

"What surprises me more is finding you here looking so wistful." He lifted her chin and forced her eyes to his. "I hoped what transpired between us would give you reason to celebrate. Our reunion will give us the power to undo all our son has wrought."

"I believe you are overlooking my absence of a physical form despite me feeling the weight of your finger against me," Delila challenged.

"Lover, I'm the usher of the undead. The docent of the departed. If I didn't have the ability to touch one's soul, I wouldn't be qualified for the position I'm in."

He leaned down and brushed his lips against where hers would be, sending a ripple of excitement through her essence. Her devil was full of tricks and secrets.

"What can we do about Drammelech? Our son has become something I can't even bare to acknowledge as mine." Shame coated her words.

"His misguided attempts to connect with me has caused immeasurable pain and suffering. As much as I wish to rectify the situation, I believe it's beyond our abilities. At this point, we may need to consider a being more powerful than ourselves."

"Such as?"

"The Great Creator."

"He exists?" Doubt clung to every questioning syllable. "If he exists, the stories about your internment must be true." She paused and considered the man she'd been connected to since before he'd walked into her barn one fine day in the early 1700's.

"The story you refer to is a simplified version of a much bigger truth, but now's not the time to get into it." He stepped away from her and pulled at the cord holding his cloak together. The fabric fell to the ground and his wings stretched out behind him. "Stay here. I'll go request an audience with one of the Guardians of the Overworld and be back before long." His strong wings beat against the air and stirred up the leaves that littered the ground of the clearing surrounding the graves.

Before long, she lost sight of him in the sky and settled her gaze back to the headstones. They had weathered the passage of time well. She ran a hand over the top of her husband's stone, knelt before it, bowed her head, and did something she'd never put stock in throughout her entire existence. Her prayer was simple and direct. Give her the strength to stop her son before he hurt more people.

She stayed there with her head rested against the smooth stone until the sound of Dema's wings on the wind reached her ears. When she stood and turned toward him another man stood beside him. Where Dema was dark and broad, the man at his side was light and slender. Dema's dark eyes blazed and the other man's silver eyes shone reminding her of the shifter Dema had inhabited. With the exception of their dark wings, the two men couldn't be more dissimilar had they tried.

"Delila, meet Nephillium. Nephillium, Delila." He gestured between them and gave a slight nod.

"This is the woman who captured your heart?" Nephillium clapped Dema on the shoulder. "I never would've expected for you to fall for one of the bewitched. One whose soul teeters so precariously between our realms." He stroked his chin and considered her with a weary stare. "Even more so, she was slated to join me even despite her dalliance with you, Demogorgon."

"Who are you to judge who I love?" Delila puffed out her cheeks and ran through the multitude of spells in her mind. She'd teach this imp a lesson if he kept up this line of discussion.

"Ah, witch, calm yourself. I judge not. I merely express my surprise. Most witches would find themselves slated for the Underworld after taking up with its leader, but somehow you managed to maintain your light." He moved closer, the sun reflecting off his bare body. "There is something quite special about you, Delila Dewsberry." He turned back to Dema and continued, "You called me here to discuss Drammelech, correct?"

"I did. He needs to be dealt with, but he's more powerful than expected. We've learned he has an artifact…"

"Fate's dagger," Delila interrupted. "My descendants have tried to procure it, but failed."

"Ah, Fate's dagger is a powerful tool, indeed." He scrubbed at his face and chewed on the corner of his lip. "Unfortunately, his possession of the dagger poses an interesting problem."

"What sort of problem?" Dema's wings bristled as irritation marred his handsome face. "Don't talk in circles, Nephillium, speak plainly."

"Fate's dagger is controlled by the guardian of human fate. Under her command the dagger can be rendered useless."

"Does that mean we need to get this woman to help us?" Delila moved closer to the men and stood to her fullest incorporeal height. "Where can we find her?"

"That's the problem I mentioned," Nephillium hedged. "She was killed some time ago, but until a replacement can be found, no one can enter the realm."

"Nephillium, I was clear. Don't talk in circles. If no one can enter the realm, how can a replacement be found?" Dema demanded, his hands bunching into fists at his sides.

"As you well know, Demogorgon, the post is filled by a human with gifts of some nature who has stood on both sides of light and dark and walked the line between them with care and discretion. Finding someone who has those qualifications isn't easy and doesn't happen often." He turned his explanation to Delila, paused, and stared deep into her being before continuing. "But your Delila more than qualifies for the job."

He winked at her, as if she was in on some long held secret, his words hung heavy in the air. Dema was the first to speak.

"No. I won't allow it."

"Don't be so hasty, old friend. Her service in the position would accomplish what you seek."

"What do you mean?" She asked, while holding up a hand to Dema's chest to halt any further objections.

"If you choose to take up the post, you will have ultimate control over Fate's artifacts—including the dagger you are concerned about." Nephillium rustled his wings and cocked his head to the side as if hearing something in the distance. "Your descendants are calling for you. It appears they require your assistance."

She turned to look over her shoulder but saw nothing.

"They can wait," Dema growled. "She won't be rushed into committing the rest of her existence to servitude."

"Time is of the essence, my friend. She'll need to decide soon. Your son has possessed the dagger for many years, I suspect. Which means it sees him as its master. Until someone takes over the post and completes the ritual, he will be in control of the dagger."

"I'll do it." The words left her mouth in a heap of syllables her brain scrambled to get out, despite her mouth's reluctance to say them.

"No. I forbid it."

"Demogorgon, it isn't your place to deny her free will."

"You didn't tell her the consequences of her choice. You failed to mention it was a life sentence. One she couldn't ever leave. It'd take an unsanctioned act of violence to end her term. And she'd never be able to travel amongst the planes. She'd be trapped in Fate's realm. Alone. Forever."

"What?" Thoughts exploded through her. How was it this agent of the light could be so underhanded while her dark lover was deemed the problem child in the hierarchy of the planes? It made no sense.

"Inconsequential. Fate's post is a high honor to a former mortal. She should be honored to be asked."

"But she wasn't asked. She was manipulated. I see some things haven't changed, old friend."

The word 'friend' grated between Dema's clenched teeth. He moved to place himself between her and Nephillium with her at his back. "Her agreement doesn't matter. She wasn't vetted by the boss."

"That's where you're wrong. She's been watched for hundreds of years. She sacrificed her love for you to save her son. The love in her heart is pure even if her son isn't. She's the perfect candidate for the post."

Delila peered at the man from around Dema's bulk and studied him closely. The twinkle in his eye was more mischievous than joyous and it worried her.

"She's agreed, Demogorgon. It's done." Nephillium clapped his hands and smiled wide.

"No. She wasn't offered compensation. You must offer her something for her sacrifice. A time limit, a plane she can visit, a corporeal body. Something. Anything." Defeat coated Dema's words.

"Don't be angry, my love." She reached a hand to her lover's face and stroked him. "It's the right thing to do. The only thing to do. Elech can never gain entry into the Overworld. Never. His death won't bring me joy, my love, but it's what must be done."

Dema lowered his head and captured her lips with his. She knew she couldn't possibly be feeling the softness of his lips or the slide of his tongue, but yet, there she found herself, in his warm embrace, enjoying what should never be. When she pulled from his embrace, she looked over her shoulder into the trees beyond this sacred place. Nephillium was gone without a sound or so much as a goodbye. But deep down, she'd be a fool to believe she'd never see him again.

Eight

Daphne

Decision made. "So where is our ghostly helper? Not that I'm eager to get possessed again," Daphne clarified as a shudder overtook her body. The duo, Dema and Delila, were the only answer to their Elech problem and if it meant being possessed again, she would do it. Although, since coming to the realization that possession was the inevitable option, Colin eyed her like she was the only glass of water in the desert. If only she could think of something witty or clever to say. Something to take the edge off the heat flaring to life inside her.

"Over there." Callie pointed toward the tree line beyond the barn.

A tall man wrapped in a dark cloak walked out into the open and her heart stuttered. "Dema." *Shit.* The devil had a body of his own now and it was as intimidating as she'd glimpsed while he'd controlled Colin in the barn.

"You can see them, too?"

"Them? I only see one person," Colin piped up. "And I'm glad to see he has a body of his own this time around."

"Delila's with him. So, I guess only one of you will need to get possessed," Callie added.

"As long as he knows I'm not up for any devilish hanky-panky," Daphne muttered under her breath. The king of the Underworld was larger than life. She had no idea how he'd fit into Colin earlier. Colin must've been on the same wavelength because he stepped to her side and slid a protective arm around her shoulder.

"I won't let him take advantage of you," he breathed in her ear.

"Promise?"

"Absolutely. I don't like to share."

The deep timbre of his possessive words sent a shiver down her spine and she swore the solid parts of her turned to lava; all molten and gooey.

"We have a solution." The air surrounding them vibrated when the devil spoke. Authority and command didn't even begin to cover his tone. Silence followed his words, but he cocked his head to the side as if listening to someone the rest of them couldn't see.

"Are you sure?" Callie asked. "Getting him to part with the dagger isn't easy. I've tried a couple of times and now he owns me like I'm a damn pet."

Colin moved them toward Jason and nudged him with his elbow. "I think your girl's lost her mind."

"Pretty sure Delila's talking. Callie can see ghosts," Jason explained.

"Delila said she has a way to take control of the dagger. It's risky and if she doesn't do it soon, Elech will win. He has everything he needs to compel Daphne." Callie waved a hand between Dema and where Delila must be standing. "If we can hold him off for long enough, Delila can take control of the dagger's power without him noticing and render it useless. It'd give us a fighting chance."

"So, what? We go in as bait?" Colin shook his head. "I'm not comfortable letting Daphne walk in there again. Remember how well that worked out the last time?"

No one had the balls to say anything. Not even Dema. Daphne cracked her neck and pulled herself to her full height. "What do I need to do?"

"Offer him what he wants. Delila says you need to make him believe you are willing to open the doors to the Overworld," Callie relayed.

Colin cast a weary glare in Callie's direction. "I'm not sure I want to blindly trust her. Last I checked, Elech still had sway over her."

"I trust Callie," Jason argued.

"Sure. You also want to get in her pants."

"Silence." Dema looked more menacing than any human ever had. "Whether you want to believe it or not, Delila has offered you pitiful humans a gift. Accept it with grace. Daphne will need to confront Drammelech and offer herself. The rest of you are unnecessary. Go about your lives and let Daphne and Delila handle this."

"Awful dismissive of you," Colin growled, his fists clenching until the sound of his joints popping echoed in the air.

"It's okay. I'll do it." Daphne stroked a hand along the ridges of his abdomen without thinking. How quickly she'd moved from shy scared single girl to intimate, caressing friend with benefits. "So, how do we get her back in me?"

"She doesn't need to inhabit you, human." Dema shook his head as if she was the dumbest human he'd ever encountered.

His rebuff stung. Who was he to make her feel bad? Hell, she'd just offered to put herself in harm's way to help control the son he created. Anger bubbled beneath the surface of her tight-lipped smile. Colin must've felt her stiffen, because he dropped his arm from her shoulders and smoothed his hand over her back in reassuring circles.

Tires on gravel shifted her focus. The dirt wafting up from beneath the tires of her brother's SUV clouded her vision.

"Get away from my sister!"

Nic stormed from the vehicle and barreled past her toward Dema.

"Nic. No!" Her words fell on deaf ears as her brother crashed into the cloaked devil. Instead of falling to the ground, Dema caught him, twisted Nic's neck in the vise of his arms. His wings spread wide, throwing his cloak back like a cape and a snarl pulled at his lips.

Nic stopped moving, frozen in the moment, breath stuck in his chest with nowhere to go, panic etched on his face.

"Let my bother go. He didn't know," she pleaded. "He's only trying to help." She threw herself forward with every intention of forcefully removing Dema's arm from around Nic's throat, but Colin grabbed her arm and held tight.

"No. Let him be."

She stood, rooted in place, the seconds ticking by slower than a day, a month. Nic's face paled as Dema lowered his head and whispered in his ear. A barely noticeable nod from Nic and Dema's arm fell away. Nic crumpled to the ground in a heap of gasps. She ran to his side and glared up at the fully exposed demon before her. With his wings spread wide and his tail flicking between his legs, there was no mistaking who was the stronger of them.

"Tell me what to do and I'll do it. Just promise my family will be safe."

"I don't make promises."

"You better if you want her to risk her life," Colin growled.

She hadn't noticed he'd moved behind her. But there he was, the man she'd fall head over heels for under any normal circumstances. Tall and broad, he exuded a power that brought her to her knees. He placed a hand on her shoulder and gave a gentle squeeze, silently commanding her to stay put.

"You demand so much from her, but offer nothing in return. In what world does that seem acceptable?" Colin challenged the devil.

"I only ask her to do what she was born to do. If shying away from her destiny is how she wants to live her life, it'll be a short one."

"I'll do it." The breathless feeling in her chest was echoed in her shaky words. "I just need a few minutes to prepare myself." She rose to her feet and smiled up at Colin. It was done. She would put her faith in Delila to rescue them all from the certain death waiting for them. Maybe she was the dumbest human alive after all.

Nine

Daphne

She should hate herself. Utterly, truly, and completely, but looking into Colin's silver eyes, Daphne couldn't think about anything other than begging him to run away with her. No turning back. No guilt. No regrets. Only the two of them together.

The feel of his big hand in hers wasn't enough as they walked back into the barn. She could hear Callie, Jason, Nic, and Dema arguing behind them, but their words didn't register. The hammering of her heart against her ribs was the only noise she could really hear. Oh, God, could Colin hear it? Shit. He had been kind enough to walk off with her, but she didn't want him to know the erratic thrum wasn't anxiety over the impending showdown with the Jersey Devil, but instead directly related to the lazy patterns his fingers traced on her hand.

"Can I ask you a question?" His voice was low and sent a shiver over her skin.

"Anything." Her answer was a breath more than a word and a flash of heat assaulted her cheeks.

"Earlier," he paused and his finger stilled mid pattern. "I know we both weren't really ourselves, but…"

"Oh. Don't worry about it," she interrupted before he could get the rest of whatever he was about to say out.

"Dema might've been in control, but I was aware," he continued still not moving. "It was your first time."

Damn it. He wasn't asking a question. He was telling her he knew and if she could, she'd melt into a puddle of liquid Daphne right here. "Really. It's not a big deal. I just hadn't gotten around to it yet." The mental head slap wasn't going to take back the lame word choice, nor was it going to take her back in time and offer a do-over.

Colin gave her hand a gentle squeeze and the gift of not making eye contact. "I know it's a big deal. And I'm sorry it happened the way it did." His words hung in the air for a second before he stammered, "It's not that I wouldn't't've wanted to do it. I mean, I'm glad I was your first—well, sorta your first. Does the fact that I was possessed take away from that?"

For the first time since he'd broached the subject, she looked at him and laughed. The awkwardness went both ways! Mr. Calm-and-Cool-Under-Pressure was just as embarrassed as she felt.

"Seriously, it's okay." She laid her hand on his arm and sighed. "I'm glad it was you even if Dema and Delila got us into this mess."

"You sure?" His eyes twinkled with mischief. "You don't feel violated or anything?"

"No. I'm just a bit embarrassed."

"Why?"

"Honestly?"

"Yeah."

"I'm kinda worried I wasn't very good." She dropped her eyes back to the ground, but before she could find a speck of dirt to fixate on, his hand was angling her head back up to meet his gaze.

"There was nothing bad about what happened between us other than the circumstances surrounding how it went down." The intensity of his stare made the heat on her face spread even lower. "If I had a say in things, it still would've happened, but there wouldn't've been Dema or Delila in the mix. And maybe we'd've seen a movie and shared a pizza or two."

"Oh." The sound barely left her lips before his descended on them in a rush of thrill and excitement. Her eyes closed and she melted into his strong embrace. This is how she always imagined it would be her first time: a hunky guy, weakness in her legs, the butterflies in her stomach the only thing keeping her upright.

"That's how our first kiss should've been." He breathed in low tones as he kissed a trail up her jaw and his tongue swirled against the ticklish spot below her ear. "After a proper date. A nice dinner.

A drive under a starry sky. All the fixings. And then if you were ready for such a big step we could've taken it farther. In a nice soft bed, and not in a dirty old barn against a wall."

"There's nothing wrong with having sex against the wall," she heard herself argue and paused. What the hell was wrong with her? It was like her hormones had taken over and she was at their mercy.

"Oh? Maybe you *do* have a little devil in you after all?"

His teasing sent her heart racing. "Maybe I do," she challenged. "Maybe we should test the theory out?"

If she could've anticipated the shocked look on his face, she would've tried to capture it on film. It looked so out of place on his handsome face that she wanted to make it happen again. Detangling her fingers from his, she stepped farther into the shadows of the old horse stall and lifted her shirt over her head. "Let's see if you have a little devil in you, too," she sing-songed as her fingers moved to the button on her jeans.

"There's nothing little about what I've got going on over here," Colin chided, amusement dancing on his every word. He moved with deliberate steps, a predator stalking his prey, hunger blazing in his eyes, the strain of restraint in every muscle she could see.

He reached her before she could wriggle the denim over her hips and placed his hands on hers, stilling the downward momentum of her pants.

"Are you sure? I don't want this time to be anything less than you making a conscious decision." He leaned down and placed a kiss on her forehead. "As much as I'd like nothing more than to have you all to myself this time, I don't want you to think this has to happen."

"Colin, I'm a grown woman. Under other circumstances, I'd take you up on the date and drive under the stars, but seeing as there's a chance I could lose when I go up against Elech today, I want there to be something I did of my own accord. A purely selfish decision. Everything I've done up until five minutes ago was about destiny and now I need time to stand still and wait for me to be ready. Ready to give away what little life I have left. So, please hear me out. Let this be about us. Just two people who want to feel alive together." She pressed a kiss to his neck and slid a hand from beneath his and pressed it against the bulge in his pants. "Pretty please? Live with me now. Let me experience love; even if it's only physical," she added in a hurried breath.

Without a word, he slid her jeans to the ground and lifted her in his arms, his lips finding hers in seconds. "There's a good chance you'll be the death of me, you know?"

"I know." She wondered if he meant this, here and now, or the upcoming fight with Elech, but quickly put the thought out of her mind as the hand not holding her to him, found the bundle of nerves at her apex. She closed her eyes and let the sensations consume her.

The warmth running through her belonged as much to the way he loved her as it did to her all-out adoration of him. As corny as it sounded in her own brain, she could feel it; his love for her. It was this intangible thing that tickled her senses and drove her wild with need, desire, passion. Like a golden little thread winding between them and securing their futures together for all eternity. A claiming of souls destined to find themselves in each other's arms.

She succumbed to the bright light his touch offered. It was a stark contrast to the darkness that had chased her since the moment of her birth. Tension coiled her muscles tight and set her nerve-endings on fire. How funny it was, finding herself here, in Colin's tender embrace all the while knowing that somewhere out there was her death, lurking, waiting in the darkness like a hungry lion stalking a gazelle.

Only she couldn't outrun the devil. She didn't stand a chance when it was her versus him. She would die. He'd use her to get what he wanted and she would be the discarded remains of her former self. Which is why even though the weight of her responsibility wasn't far from notice, all she wanted was the pleasure Colin's hands provided. Unlike the snap-back-to-reality sex with Dema in Colin's body, this was tame, gentle, sweet even. He laid her on the ground, met her eyes, offered her a crooked smile, and sank out of view.

'Giving' should be the man's middle name considering how intent he was on making his time between her legs memorable. An unleashed nervous chuckle slipped between her lips and Colin stilled with his tongue pressed firmly to her clit. Over the rise of her breasts, their eyes met. A wicked smile tugged at the corners of his mouth and his fingers plunged deep, a finger fest of stroking, coaxing, reaching, until there was no chance of her laughing. Her breath, short pants of joy as he brought her to the edge of the precipice, echoed in the stall.

The tension built to a fever. She needed this. This climax. This sense of wantonness. This freedom. Because this time it would be her choice. Not Delila's. This orgasm would be hers and hers alone; as all first one's should be. Not that there hadn't been plenty of opportunities over the last twenty five years, but none of those men had made her want to give up control long enough to have sex with them let alone climax. Colin wasn't like other men. The proof was in the way he paid attention to each movement she made, the sounds emanating from her of their own accord. He nipped and kissed her skin like it was a treat to be savored and she wanted for nothing more than to lose herself into this man even under these completely odd circumstances. She wanted this moment of normal. This breath of being fully aware and alive.

He stilled, took a deep breath, and shifted right before her very eyes into a mocha-tinted cloud, his clothes falling to the ground beneath where he'd been. In the next blink of an eye, he was solid and reached for her hands. Silently purposeful yet demanding, he raised her hands above her head and intertwined his fingers with hers. He paused long enough for her to smile before he slid home.

The cliff he'd been building to, rushed up to meet her and she crossed it in a scream. Fully unleashed, she savored every hurried beat of her heart hammering against her ribcage while Colin increased his pace, determination and wonder mixed on his handsome face. She raised her head the scant few inches required to press her lips to the pulse point in his neck when he found his release.

He stilled, his weight a source of warmth and comfort against her. She savored every second of their matching heartbeats and sighed.

"That was how your first time should've been," he whispered in her ear before sliding out of her body. "I know it doesn't change how it went down, but hopefully it doesn't leave you with the same sense of 'ick' that the possession did."

Ick? What was he trying to say? Her face burned and the threat of tears pulsed behind her eyes. Was this pity sex? A "sorry about that time I accidentally fucked you while possessed?" Squirming from beneath him, she stood, and stepped into her jeans. There wasn't any room left in her heavy heart to deal with more emotional scars today. Not with her death looming.

"You okay?"

She glanced over her shoulder and relished the confused look on his face. Served him right. "Yup. I'm fine. Just need to get my head on straight." She slipped her shirt on and walked away from him without giving it another thought. There wasn't anything more to say. Not anymore.

Ten

Delila

No sooner had Daphne and Colin disappeared into the barn did Delila spy the visage of Nephillium off in the distance. The feeling of déjà vu bled into full color reality and the lump in her throat solidified. Dema and the others stood in heated debate as she silently slid away from Dema and stepped toward the angel.

He nodded for her to follow him deeper into the trees. "It's time."

She hated his matter-of-fact way of speaking. "I know." She twisted her hands and wondered how Dema would react when he found her gone. "What do I do?"

"Sign here." A rolled parchment appeared in one hand.

She unrolled it and scanned the words penned in blood-red ink. A contract. One that bound her to the post of Fate for an unknown timeframe. She'd control the futures of all the inhabitants on Earth and as negotiated by Dema, himself, be granted access to both the Overworld and Underworld. An asterisk loomed ominously above the clause. She read to the bottom and found the caveat to the negotiation. While she would have access to both planes, she would have to choose only one. Forever. So spend her days working as Fate and her nights tangled in Dema's embrace in the Underworld? Was anything about that appealing? She cocked her head and gave Nephillium a weary glare.

"I see your boss is intent on punishing Dema and I for eternity."

"Hardly." He shook his head then sent his wings wide. "It's been agreed upon that you will have access none other in the position was ever granted." His words were pert, but his face belayed an openness she didn't expect from him.

"Alright. Where do I sign?"

A dagger appeared in his hand as the scroll had and he passed it to her. "At the bottom. A few drops is all that is required."

"I'm a ghost. Pretty sure the idea of me signing in blood died a long time ago," she challenged.

"Yet, you are holding the scroll." He passed her the blade, "and a sacred knife," he added with a smirk.

The instrument was solid and heavier in her grasp than she would've imagined it could be. She slid her index finger along its edge and a thin trail of crimson followed in its wake. No sooner had a few drops landed on the page in thick blots, the trees surrounding them disappeared and she found herself staring at solid walls.

The scroll and dagger went the way of the woods and she took a slow turn around the room. It had a familiar feel to it, but she knew she'd never set hide nor hair in the place with the magical hum. She walked the space and took in every opulent detail. With every footfall she felt her destiny seal, an unsettling certainty in her stomach. There was no turning back now.

She walked to one of the many doors tucked around the room, opened it and behind the door awaited a decadent bedroom. She sat on the edge of the bed and ran her hand over the satiny coverlet. Every soft surface screamed otherworldly comfort, as if they were made from clouds in the Overworld and hand-spun by angels.

"There's more to see."

She hadn't seen Nephillium leaning against the doorframe until he spoke. She considered him. He was the anti-Dema if ever she'd seen one. He exuded light and grace in every moment, but unlike the darkness that Dema wore with pride, she could sense her Overworld guide hid his darkness deep down where it was easily overlooked. She twirled a strand of hair around her finger and luxuriated in the ability to do so. It had been hundreds of years since she last had a body of her own. She peered around the room for a mirror, but there wasn't a single one.

"You don't have need of a mirror," Nephillium answered her unasked question. "Nor will you have any other human needs. It's one of the perks of the job." He raised an eyebrow.

"Great. No waiting in long lines to use the restroom, as they do these days." The snarky words sent his eyebrow farther into his forehead. It was nice to know she still had the ability to be herself in some small way.

He stood back and ushered her from her new sanctuary. "The most important room is this way," he said and gestured toward a door.

He stepped back and waited for her to reach for the handle. So much for his gentlemanly persona.

"The door will only open for the one who has signed the scroll," he explained.

"Can you stop answering questions I don't ask you?" She glared at him and reached her fingers toward the knob.

"On this plane, it's even harder to tell what you speak aloud from what you think in your head. Without any other noise to distract my abilities, there's no ignoring the words floating through my mind." He shrugged.

The gesture looked silly on the Overworld Guardian. *So can everyone in the Overworld read minds?* She thought and waited, hand stilled on the knob.

Only those slated to become Guardians. He sent the answer mentally. *And as Fate, you can have the ability to hear thoughts as long as you concentrate while in the presence of a mortal being or another Guardian.*

So it's an Overworld gift? She studied him while she waited for his response.

There are humans walking the earthen plane that also have the ability.

His careful answer piqued her curiosity. "Really? Why?" The mental conversation was unnerving.

"Because it helps them hone their gifts before they ascend to Guardian status after their human death."

Human Guardians in training? A chill raced up her spine. How was she to oversee all these people? People she didn't even know existed. She leaned in, turned the knob, and stepped over the threshold into a chamber of sorts. As far as she could see, rows and rows of ornately carved wooden shelves ran through the room. Every shelf was lined with stacks and stacks of rolled parchments. She fingered the edge of one scroll and removed it from a shelf near the entrance of the room. With a turn of her hand it unrolled in her grasp.

Print leaked onto the paper before her eyes as if only made for her to read. She scanned the document to the bottom and felt the color drain from her face. The scroll belonged to a new life that was only recently created and its fate was already written. A child was to be born in eight and half months under the noonday sun to a young mother, alone and afraid. And the child would be the one thing to save the mother from herself.

A fluttering in her chest where her heart should be surprised her and made her hands shake. She

71

rolled the scroll and set it on the closest shelf she could reach as to not drop it from her quaking hands.

"Careful where you return the scrolls," Nephillium chided. "They all have a designated spot and if returned to a wrong one or disturbed, it can upset the balance. He pointed to a shelf one up from where she had placed the rolled parchment. "It belongs there."

"Do you know what it said?" She moved the scroll to the shelf he pointed to. "Why am I asking? Of course you know." A shake of her head cleared her brain as she fought to digest what she'd just learned.

"Actually, I don't know what they say. As a Guardian, I can't read them and when you think about what you've read, I can't hear your thoughts. Propriety information and all I suppose."

His unfazed look did little to convince her. She was positive he was curious about the contents of the rolled parchment. She turned away from the shelf and noticed the documents in this area all had symbols on the outside edges. "What do those stand for?"

"What?"

"The symbols." She tapped a finger to anther scroll below the bright red flickering symbol that wavered as a white wave washed over it.

"I can't see any symbols. I'm sure as you read more of the scrolls, their meanings will become apparent." He paused and a look of uncertainty washed over his face as he must've contemplated his next words. "Were there symbols on the other one?"

She looked back at the first scroll she'd read and weighed her options. "Why do you ask?"

He narrowed his eyes, whether at her or in an attempt to see what remained hidden from his purview she wasn't sure.

"Merely curious. The contents of that one appeared to trouble you."

A quick sweep of her eyes showed only two scrolls in the near vicinity with the dark feather. But the one she had read also had the white streams that appeared to wash over the feather. But on closer inspection, she could see something she hadn't noticed before; a faint yellow ray of light etched behind the feather as it waved in the breeze. There was something compelling about the way the symbols interacted as if alive on the paper. Something magical. Beautiful. Hauntingly so.

She watched the feather twirl in the wind on the page and from beneath the feather, slithered a green serpent. After reading the contents, its appearance made complete sense. Another shiver wracked her body. The beam of light darkened and faded away as the snake reared back as if ready to strike from the page.

Delila shook the thought away and turned back to Nephillium. "I only asked because it seems some have more than one symbol."

"That's a result of the last catastrophe here. When *your* son stole the dagger. He also upset some of the scrolls which set the world askew. It will be your job to set things right."

"How so?"

"You have the ability to change the course of life for any being on the earthen plane. See that basin over there?" He pointed a slender finger toward a gold bowl simmering with a flame down the aisle. "It acts as an equalizer of sorts. If a scroll finds its way into the flame you see, it will change the course of the destiny and set about the end of the being's existence."

"How can you sound so matter-of-fact about someone's life? 'Just drop it in the fire and get rid of the problem?' I can't imagine the creator wants me to kill off his creations." Her eyes returned to the shelved scroll; her motherly protective instinct reflex hard at work. "I won't go about killing people for sport."

"It's part of your contract," Nephillium replied, his tone tense despite the neutral set of his face. "The wrongs your son caused need to be rectified."

Every cell in her body warned, instead of arguing, she needed to remove him from this room. Immediately. "I see." She brushed past him and headed for the door, careful to make sure he didn't touch anything as he followed behind her.

She returned to the antechamber and selected another door. This one opened at the mere thought of entering and once over the threshold she felt more at home than she had anywhere else in all her existence.

An apothecary of sorts was laid out before her. A solid plank of wood table stood vigil in the center with a small stool tucked beneath. Shelves lined the walls full of ingredients, potions, everything a witch could want. The only thing missing was a spell book. She scoured the shelves and table, finding loose parchment with scribbled spells, but not a complete book of shadows.

Maybe like the rooms she'd already been through, this one was waiting for her. She turned and found two matching doors at the rear of the room. They stood side by side, identical in appearance except the one on the left had a smudge or something in the wood midway down. She neared the doors with caution as sounds and smells behind the left one assaulted her senses.

The other stood silent, a beam of light peeking beneath the wooden edge. She reached for the knob of the second door. As it swung inward, she was greeted by the stern face of Nephillium. She swung around so quickly that she almost lost her balance. Mere seconds ago, he'd been standing right behind her.

"So this is your choice?"

"I don't understand" Confusion mixed with dread and settled deep in her core as the meaning of his words washed over her like a tidal wave. This was it. This was the choice the contract had alluded to. A defiant shake of her head was all she could manage before she slammed the door in his angelic face.

The door to her left beckoned her.

"You may only choose one door to remain. That choice will be permanent and overwrite all you've done in all your past lives. Overworld versus Underworld. The choice is yours."

Nephillium again stood behind her. She swung around and her glare landed as planned.

"You're manipulating the terms. Dema wouldn't hear of it. However, no choice needs to be made right now." She straightened her spine and bumped him with her shoulder as she brushed past him.

Back in the main room, her eyes landed on an orb. Curiosity took hold. One glance in its murky surface told her more than she could've imagined. Dema, hidden amongst darkened shadows in the woods. Pacing. Predicting. Planning his next move.

A dull thu-thunk echoed in her chest. A mirrored beating of Dema's heart. She concentrated on the harsh angles of his face and a whirlwind of thoughts pelted her brain. Her true love was ready. Ready to put aside every bit of legend, every wrong he'd clung to, every ounce of his pride. He would snuff out what his love for her had created. He would retire to the Underworld without regret, secure in the knowledge that their love could bloom anew for all of eternity. And he would do it all without risking a single piece of another mortal's soul because he knew it would please her. *Delila*.

Her name flowed through her own head and a ripple of joy seeped from it, unfettered and free. Before she could take too much pleasure in the moment, Nephillium appeared in the woods before Dema's eyes. Eyes she realized she now saw through. Her breath caught and she whirled around to confirm his absence from her chamber.

"She has chosen, brother." The Guardian's words, mere taunts, echoed off the trees. "What choice is yours?"

Delila peered back into the orb. How dare Nephillium taunt Dema so? He knew her choice was Dema and yet here he stood claiming the opposite. A scream ripped from her core and bounced around the empty room. Her fingernails bit into the sensitive flesh of her palms as she tried to conjure herself into existence on the Earthen plane. How hard could it be? Closing her eyes and concentrating didn't work, nor did a litany of spells from her memory.

It was the low, deep tone of Dema's voice that stilled her.

"My fate was written long ago. She was never meant to be mine."

Without waiting to hear anymore, she ran. Away from the orb. Away from the room. Away from everything she had agreed to. It wasn't until she stood before the door that lead to the Underworld did it all begin to make sense to her. She wasn't running away from her destiny. She was running toward it. Toward Dema. Toward love.

Without preamble, her hand landed on the heated doorknob. It twisted in her grasp with only the gentlest of turns. There wasn't time to think even though Nephillium's words flittered through her mind as the door opened before her. No. She had to reassure Dema. He would always be her choice. Always.

One foot in front of the other was all it took to seal her fate. Refusing to look back, Delila squared her shoulders and crossed the threshold into Hell.

Eleven

Delila

THE THING ABOUT the Underworld—it wasn't all fire and brimstone. Sure, there was a fair share of sulfur smell and the heat a few notches below blistering, but it wasn't exactly what Delila expected.

Not that anyone, not even Dema, had ever given her much to expect when crossing into the plane. The Underworld looked a lot like the rest of the world; condos, homes, buildings. Sure, screams echoed off walled surfaces, but it was pretty much like any other place she'd ever experienced. Just hotter.

Unlike the Overworld, there wasn't anyone waiting to greet her at the door, so she stepped through unassisted. As she walked the heated brick walkway, unseen fingers grabbed at her, pulling, pinching. Howls wrapped around her as she walked through the streets, caressing her, calling her closer. When she did see someone, she asked where she could find Dema, the king, and was rewarded with a toothless smile and a hand gesture she hadn't before seen. But when he winked and waved her along toward the biggest building in town, she followed without hesitation.

If Dema had returned here after his conversation with Nephillium, he'd be surprised to see her. They could continue their reunion and work out the details of their plot for Elech. Without the Overworld as an option, she decided to make the most of her choice. She'd luxuriate in Dema's realm as often as possible and it would give her the peace her soul needed.

Determined, she entered the building. Standing guard were three demon-like creatures who snapped razor sharp teeth in her direction.

She straightened herself to her full height and calmed the butterflies in her gut. "I'm here for Dema."

"Who dares call the king by name?" Bright eyes flashed from the demon who spoke.

"His queen." She prided herself in the lack of quiver in her voice. "Tell him Delila is here." She stared down the demons until all three dropped their eyes from hers. One picked up a com and spoke into it an otherworldly dialect.

"He's not in, but you can go wait in his private chambers. His assistant will show you in."

One of the creatures, moved from behind the counter and led her toward a bank of elevators. When the bell dinged signaling the cars approach, he stepped back and bowed, his tail flicking along the ground as she stepped into the car. He reached a long finger in and pressed the button marked B-5 before receding from her view.

When the lift stopped at the bottom, the doors parted and she stepped into a gallery of some sort. Wall to wall easels stood with different sized canvases full of similar styled artwork all depicting a woman who she would swear was her. Blond curls bounced around a youthful face and bright blue eyes sparkled as a coy smile lit the lips of the subject. Another canvas boasted sleepy eyes and a pale pink glow spread across the cheeks, while the subject's lips parted in swollen invitation.

"He's thought of you every day since you cursed him."

She hadn't noticed the short, elfish man when she exited the elevator, but now that she saw him, it was hard to imagine she had missed him. He stood only about four feet tall, but was shrouded in a dapper tuxedo as if on his way to a fancy evening out, rather than waiting around for Dema to return.

"Why are you here and not in the Overworld celebrating with the master?"

"Celebrating?" The confusion she saw on his face surely matched the confusion on her very own. "Has something happened?"

"He's been reappointed to the post he's dreamed of so often since meeting you. Your salvation, the day he saved you knowing it could end his existence, he earned his way into the Overworld."

Dema hadn't thought to mention he was no longer the ruler of the Underworld. Why? "When did this happen?"

"Only today was he notified. There's much cause for celebration. He's been particularly grumpy since your curse." A raised eyebrow taunted her. "Which begs the question… why are you here?"

She turned toward the elevator, her feet ready to flee, but the entrance disappeared before her very eyes, abandoning her in this shrine of sorts.

"It's written that you've chosen, Mistress Fate. There's no going back. Not now. Not ever."

*****

There was nothing more to do. Nothing to keep her here in this Hell. Her one true love was gone. Delila fell to the floor and sobbed.

"Missus, the sooner you come to terms with your situation, the sooner you can move on," the impish man chided.

How dare he scold her like a child. Everything was wrong. There was nothing more for her here. Or on the earthen plane. Not even in her new home. Her son was determined to erase all the good she had brought into existence and she was destined to suffer in loneliness for the rest of her existence.

A hand landed gently on her shoulder. "He wouldn't want you to be sad, Missus. He'd want you to forge ahead."

"Still, he never thought to mention his new appointment."

"If there is anything I can tell you with certainty, it's that the master always has another plan. Trust that this is true and find solace in his love for you."

Unlike the air around them, his touch was cool. Soothing. Calming. Delila, swallowed back her anguish and met the man's eyes. "Thank you. Your kindness is appreciated. I'm sure Dema will miss you greatly."

"Ah, but you will always have my council, Missus. For I'll be at your beck and call should you need anything within the realm. Call Aaró and I'll meet you at the gates." He bowed low and backed away, out of sight.

Determined to do Dema proud, she rose to her feet, threw back her shoulders, and raised her chin. She would get through this. She would do whatever it took to save her lineage. As the thoughts settled in her soul, the elevator doors appeared and opened, as if waiting for her.

Her fortitude faltered as she walked the pathway back toward her realm. Loneliness crept up her spine and tickled her nerve endings until a wave of nausea erupted. She paused long enough on the brick pathway to retch. The emptiness inside was bigger somehow than it ever had been before.

She was stuck. Stuck in this in-between. Stuck with orders to kill people. Stuck alone.

Her feet refused to move forward, her legs threatened to collapse. The joy she'd felt only a brief time ago had been fully replaced with despair. Heartache. Emptiness.

"Why are you here, witch?"

Every fiber of her being sprang to life. She'd recognize his voice anywhere. She'd spent her entire human existence waiting for him. "I think the more important question is, what are you doing here?" She turned and looked up into Dema's dark eyes. "I was told you'd changed posts."

His lip pulled up at the corner. "For you, my love. I was given another chance for you. For us."

"And I'm here. Stuck in the Underworld for the rest of eternity." Her voice stuck in her throat and her final word was little more than a croak. "Alone."

"No!" His roar shook the foundations of the buildings surrounding them. "It can't be true. Nephillium was instructed to tell you."

"Oh, he told me plenty. However, your promotion seemed to escape his memory." She shook the tears away. "Dema, I agreed to this post for you. For the chance at an eternity together. And now…" She flung herself into his arms, "And now, he's asked me to do unspeakable things."

Dema rubbed a soothing hand against her back as his wings encircled them. "While there are some parts of his requests that seem unreasonable, I'm sure others are necessary."

She wrenched from his grasp. "No. Not you too. I won't terminate innocents." She glared at the devil before her. "I can't believe you are even asking this of me. Some are our kin; the evidence of our love." Without waiting for his response, she turned on her heel and stomped away.

On the edge of her sightline, a door appeared as if only for her. The door that would lead back to her apothecary and chamber. The door away from Dema and the future she had wanted for them. The door that only she could access.

"Delila. Stop."

She ignored his command and picked up her pace.

"Please."

She caught her foot on a brick and stumbled. Dema didn't beg. Ever.

"Give me one good reason," she challenged, without turning back to face him.

"I'll give you as many as you need, so long as you hear me out." He paused and she could sense his ever nearing presence. "The evidence of our love has resulted in terrible tragedies," he began, his breath ticking her ear. "But it also ended with much joy and love. Look at Daphne. Whether she admits it or not, she's found her true love in that shifter. Just as you found your true love in me."

His hands caressed her shoulders and his lips feathered along the sensitive skin beneath her jaw.

"Even the happiness our love has brought about, Nephillium can order me to terminate." Pants of breath mixed in the hot, heavy air around them. She dared not succumb to the burning need within. "We must do something."

"I am doing something," Dema chided. "I'm reminding you to trust me. We will go to Daphne and ready her for battle. She's willing to help. Willing to sacrifice. And it will be our duty to ensure the sacrifice made isn't hers."

He stopped his hot-lipped assault on her skin and stepped beside her and slid her hand in his.

"Do you truly believe we stand a chance of winning? Elech is so much stronger than either of us." She worried her lip between her teeth and clutched his hand as if it were the only thing tethering her to this plane.

"Together, we can do anything." He raised her hand to his lips and a kiss burned her skin. "Trust me."

Crossing back into her chamber was anticlimactic at best until she realized Dema crossed beside her. A single thread of hope unraveled in her gut.

"Wait here and I'll see to Daphne and her friends. I'll bring them here and we can formulate a plan."

"I have a better idea. Go to Elech. Offer him what he's always wanted. The chance to stand beside you and take the Overworld by force. Bring him here, to me, and we can coax him into the Underworld."

"Our son will not believe I've had such a change of heart. It's better to prepare Daphne before we involve Elech," Dema argued.

A door behind him creaked open and the witch, Jason, appeared in the doorway. "Oh," he chirped. "I didn't expect anyone to be here. The other times I visited…" his voice trailed off as his eyes registered who stood before him.

"How did you get in here?"

Delila's thoughts shot from Dema's mouth before she could even complete the thought.

"A book in the Daily Dews led me here." Jason braced himself.

"What?" Dema exploded. "How is it that a mere witch can just walk right into the Overworld's most sacred place?"

"I'm sure there's a perfectly good explanation for it," she soothed, and rubbed her hand against Dema's arm. "Was it a book of shadows?"

Jason nodded.

"Where is it?" She held out her hand for the book.

"Not here. But it's safe," he replied. He turned to Dema. "Daphne, Nic, and Callie are ready. I've removed the spells cloaking Callie to draw Elech to the Dews. When he arrives, Daphne and Callie will direct him into this room. If I'm not mistaken, those are the doors he's been looking for." He pointed to the rear of the room, paused, and cracked his knuckles. "Nic, Colin, and I will stay out of sight when they cross the threshold, but once they cross with Elech, so will we." He rolled his head on his neck. "Daphne will pretend to struggle to open the doors and then when he's not watching, Nic and I will wrestle him into the Underworld, where you can deal with him."

His last phrase was aimed at Dema.

"No." Delila moved toward the witch. I have an idea. Just give me a moment."

"Time isn't a luxury we have, my love," Dema whispered. "Knowing our son, he's already nearby and will beat down the doors to the Overworld before you could so much as create a new spell."

She whirled and met him head on. "It's time for you to trust me." A quick kiss on his lips punctuated her unspoken demand.

Without waiting for a response from either man, she raced from the room. An eerie glow emanated from the orb in the antechamber, but she didn't slow her stride to investigate. She burst through the door to the records room and went right toward the shelves she'd seen earlier.

If she could find the right scroll, no one would have to get hurt. She could do what should've been done long ago. Careful not to misplace any of the rolled parchments, she gently picked through the rolls, looking for the symbol she could only assume was meant to be her son's. The dark emblem called to her as if it knew she was searching for it. She pulled the scroll from its place on the shelf and unwound it. Sure enough, it belonged to Drammelech. She read through the contents to the bottom, and a lump formed in her throat. Her hand stilled as her eyes landed on a scroll that glowed with a slight golden glimmer. Even though she knew Dema's patience wouldn't last long, she caressed the edge of the second paper. It warmed beneath her touch and the feathery beating erupted in her chest again.

A quick peek wouldn't hurt, right? Besides why else would this scroll glow unlike the others? Maybe it contained what she needed to combat the revelation she'd seen in Elech's future.

She removed the rolled parchment from its place and it unraveled with her touch. She scanned the document. The thudding in her chest echoed in her ears as understanding collided with heartbreak. The sacrifices she'd made for her son were far from over, if the scroll was to be believed. She rewound the parchment, slid both under her arm, and did the only thing she could think of.

The bowl of fire flickered before her. If Nephillium was to be believed, this flame was the cleansing fire of Fate. Delila passed a hand over the flames. Unlike a typical fire, this gave off no heat. She dipped her head and peered into the cone of blue centered within the blaze. However, if she destroyed only one of the two scrolls in her hand, it would still leave a gaping hole in the fabric of the future.

One flick of her wrist and her tormented indecision would end. All she needed was one spark of bravery. Not even a full-fledged blaze was required. Only the tiniest iota would do. She inhaled a calming breath, faced the fire head on and readied the scrolls. An image of Dema, his wings spread wide, arms open and waiting, flashed in her mind. This was the best thing to do. She had to believe it. Even if it meant never falling into Dema's winged embrace again. She had to do this. She had to give the people she had sworn to protect this one last gift.

Her hand shook, but her resolve was strong.

An agonizing scream ripped through the chamber and broke her concentration. Elech had found them. She dropped the scrolls to the floor and raced from the room. Time was up.

Twelve

Drammelech

Daphne.

ALL HIS patience had led to this moment and Elech refused to even consider failure as an option.

When his hold on the witch had snapped, he knew it was only a matter of time before the humans tried something. But he never expected to find them huddled in the ransacked bookshop again. Would they never learn? No amount of books could help them beat him.

Sure, Callie, the witch, had somehow broken from his control. But he still had something more important to Daphne. He steepled his fingers and watched the animated exchange between the humans within the confines of the store.

What was he waiting for? He had never been one to let an opportunity pass without taking what he desired. His bloodstained hands were proof of that. Elech cracked his neck and took the necessary steps into the Daily Dews.

"I hear you've been looking for me," he sing-songed. "Your poor mother was just begging me to save your soul, *Daphne*." Her name blossomed on his tongue like a fragrant fruit he'd been refused in the past; sacred and sweet. "Although, dear old Hope isn't long for this world."

"No."

Daphne's voice tickled his ears and coaxed a smile from him.

"I'm afraid so. Once you perform your duties as promised all those years ago, I'll release her soul. It's too bad that her body isn't nearby though." He shook his head for emphasis. "A bodiless soul tends to get sucked into the Underworld pretty quick. All those hungry demons, waiting for fresh, innocent, souls."

"No. You can't do that to her." Only a hint of her former bravado existed in her shaking words. She whirled toward the witch. "Call dad. Tell him to get mom and bring her here. Now!"

"Ah, silly girl," Elech chided. "It's not that simple. You need to first open the door to the Overworld. That was the agreed upon terms of your mother's sacrifice. So, don't go getting any ideas of crossing me, because mommy-dear will be mine forever if things go awry." He couldn't keep the smile from playing across his face as his eyebrow arched to punctuate his position of power.

"I'll do it."

Whispered words. Words he never thought he'd so simply hear. "What?" He needed to be certain.

"I'll do it. I'll open the gates of the Overworld. Just promise you won't hurt anyone else."

An almost imperceptible nod acted as his agreement. "Come. Now." He walked toward where he had seen the male witch disappear. "Ah, what do we have here?" The irritating witch crossed the threshold as he approached. He'd had more than enough of this man's meddling.

Elech's dual-tipped tongue flickered from his mouth and savored the taste of fear in the air. His hand shot out like a dart and grabbed the one the humans called Jason by the throat. "Lead on," he demanded and dragged Jason behind him into a place he'd frequented many moons ago. He was almost home.

Thirteen

Daphne

In Daphne's experience, all of the best plans had unintended consequences, and this one was sure to be no different. Callie and Jason had concocted this harebrained idea, and now, she had been thrust through the barrier of the real world into a strange place. Jason was firmly clutched in the Jersey Devil's grip and Colin crouched half-hidden behind a bookshelf in the Daily Dews, Callie's occult bookstore and coffee shop, giving her silent hand signals.

Perched on his toes, like a tiger waiting to pounce at the slightest sign of her distress, Colin shook away her unspoken pleas to help Jason. Elech must've sensed him hiding there, because before she could even get the word across her lips, she watched, helpless as the blade they needed flew through the air and slashed across Colin's handsome face.

"No!" Daphne's voice housed more power in one small word than any combination she could've formed. Her entire existence exhaled as she watched blood pour from his wound and his being scattered into thousands of tiny light particles in slow motion.

"Did you really think that human could keep me from you?" Elech sneered and stepped over the threshold, dragging Jason's almost limp body with him.

Nic moved to where Colin had been standing only seconds ago. In his place wavered a chocolate brown cloud.

Every step Elech took toward her destiny, sent her heartbeat on a faster track. With a wave of his hand, the dagger soared back into his hand. The door between the planes closed and she stood rooted to the ground. Jason's body fell to the floor in a heap. Now it was up to her. Her and Elech. The Jersey Devil was finally getting his wish; her trapped with him in the only place he wanted to be.

"Drammelech, you don't have to do this."

Daphne's legs threatened to betray her as Dema's voice washed over her. There was no worse of a situation she could imagine beyond this one. Surrounded by the two most powerful beings she had ever known and nowhere to go. No one to help. Nothing left to hope for.

She closed her eyes and said a silent prayer for Colin, hoping the haze of color she'd seen before the door had cut her off from her only hope of rescue was one of his many visages.

"Father." Elech stepped over Jason's body and gave it a small kick.

Elech's curt tone did little to sway Daphne.

"Son, please. I know you think this is what I want, but you don't have to do this. Things have changed."

"It's the only way to ensure your place, Father. Our greatness. Living hidden among humans has done little to redeem them. And those who think those puny beings are somehow more worthwhile and cherished than gods like us, deserve what they get. I've waited far too long not to follow through. I've made deal after deal." He waved his hand in Daphne's direction. "I've done things to make you proud and ensure I'd be strong enough to do whatever it took for us to assume our rightful place high among the immortals, where all beings cower at our feet. Tremble in fear over our power. Bow before us. Things you spoke of so long ago. Things I promised to make come true. Hell, you stand here today because of what I've accomplished."

"Drammelech, you're misguided."

"Misguided? I'm fulfilling your will." Confusion rolled over the Jersey Devil's face.

"And I take full responsibility for your misdeeds."

Was Dema seriously pleading with him? The spark of hope at hearing his voice died a quick death deep in Daphne's chest. If Dema's plan was to reason with Elech, they would all die.

"Misdeeds?" Elech shook his head and clenched the dagger in his hand until his knuckles whitened. "You've gone soft over the years. Wasn't it you who taught me the value of a human's soul? The power a soul freely given could allow one such as ourselves to wield? The sweetness a soul of someone so desperate they'd give it away for something as insignificant as love?"

Dema's wings flew out to their full breadth, and Daphne dropped to the floor. There was no way in hell she was about to be collateral damage in a fight between the two devils. Sure, she'd signed up to sacrifice herself if it would ensure her family's safety, but demon fighting was not a sport she's had any interest in participating in. She crawled beneath the safety of a large table that stood in the middle of the room. It was her first opportunity to really take a good look at the chamber. Jason had warned her that she'd need to buy some time once she made it to the rear of the room where the doors to the other realms stood.

A feigned struggle with the door should've bought Jason, Colin, and Nic the time to overpower Elech, rescue her, and somehow convince Elech to wander into the Underworld where Dema could imprison him for the rest of forever. Too bad Jason might be dead only steps away from where she hid, Colin may lay just as dead on the other side of the now nonexistent door to the Dews and Nic was on the other side. She was more screwed than she'd ever been and there was nothing she could do about it.

Daphne tuned out the commotion between the devils and turned her eyes to the matching doors at the rear of the room and studied them for any decipherable markings that would lead her to the correct door. The more she stared, the more the

97

door on the left called to her. If an inanimate object could call to someone, this door was doing it. A slight golden glow radiated from beneath the solid pane.

On hands and knees, she dared crawl from the safety of her cover. Instinct drew her forward, toward the now glistening door. Before she made much headway toward her destination, a strong hand grabbed her hair and yanked. Dema's body fell to the floor, the dagger parked in his chest. Panic chased any rational thought away. *Shit.*

"It's time, Key. Unlock the door. Now." Elech's hot breath washed over her skin while hatred clung to every exposed bit of her body.

Don't say anything.

Startled, Daphne looked for Delila and winced at Elech's unrelenting hold on her hair.

I'm just in the other room. Speak if you can hear me.

The barest of movements fought against Elech's grip and she yelped.

Good. Lead him to the doors. I'll find a way to let the witches in. Together we should be able to spell him into submission for long enough that Dema can wrestle him into the Underworld.

Daphne waited for fear to take hold as she stood before the matching doors under his allowance. In the back of her mind, Delila spoke to her, a constant whisper she couldn't ignore.

The door to the left. The one with the symbol carved in it. That's the one.

Daphne wanted to yell at her. Demand she shut up. Beg her to listen. Explain that Dema couldn't help. Not with the dagger in his chest. Daphne spared a quick glance back at the king of the Underworld and was relieved to see Jason slowly coming around.

Before she could even make a move toward either door, a commotion at the other end of the room erupted. Nic and Colin burst through the door like avenging angels. In the Dews, she could see Callie on the floor. Whatever they had done to open the door must've caused a great deal of energy on her part. Colin stopped beside Dema and attempted to remove the dagger.

This wasn't the time to contemplate it though.

"Open it. Now," Elech growled and shoved her toward the doors.

Tears streamed down her face and a whimper careened from her lips. Her scalp screamed. His hold on her hair warred with the force of her body being shoved forward.

"Leave her alone. She'll do it, just leave her alone." Nic, ever faithful, ever by her side, ever determined to save her from herself and the damn devil, pushed forward. "Please. Take me if you need, but leave her alone."

He slid his hand into hers and squeezed.

Unsure if he was brave or stupid for demanding to come with her, she returned his grip. Daring the devil to kill him where he stood had been horrible.

She raised a hand toward first the glowing door on the left as Delila insisted, then swung it to the other. Daphne hissed. The second door physically pained her to even consider touching. Daphne wanted to ask, but she knew her witchy ancestor wouldn't tell. But it was odd, how eerily quiet Delila was in her head. Daphne returned her hand to her side.

"Stop stalling." Elech's words carried a bite that made her quake. "Open the door."

"I'm not exactly sure how this works," she rebuked. "Am I supposed to know which one leads to the Overworld?"

"The prophecy states the female heir would only be welcome in the Overworld. One door should call to you." He paused long enough to point a finger between the two doors. "Which one is it?"

Daphne, change of plans. Open the door on the right. Nephillium and his army are ready...

She reached her hand back to the doors. If she could tune out Delila's new yammering in her head, she could feel a pulse beyond each door. One beat with fear while the other expelled heat and... was that desire? *Huh.* She placed a steady hand on the smooth wooden pane of each, gauging the energy behind it. To her right, the despair grew heated beneath her fingers, warning her away, while on the left, the coaxing and cajoling begged her to turn the knob.

Behind one door she prayed the Guardian, Nephillium, stood, ready with his army, waiting to defeat Elech. His name was constantly running through her head in Delila's voice as if she was trying to conjure him with her thoughts. The second door would lead to the Underworld. A place where souls wandered aimless and tortured. A place where those she loved could be taken hostage. A place where there would be no victory for any of them.

She withdrew her hands and contemplated the doors. Despite Delila's insistence on the door to the right, it felt all wrong. Nothing beyond that door rang of the peace and tranquility Nephillium had boasted. Not even close. Maybe Delila was wrong. Sure, she seemed to have knowledge of this magic chamber and the doors it housed, but maybe she made a mistake.

"Select the door that will lead us to the Overworld," Dema called from his place on the floor.

The depth of his voice rumbled through her, putting each nerve ending on high alert. Delila trusted him, but not a single piece of her did. Add to it, his weakened state and she had little confidence in the king of all evil.

"It's okay Daph. I'm right here with you," Nic soothed and placed a hand on her shoulder. "You've got this."

His reassuring smile gave her the strength she needed. She grasped the knob Delila insisted would save them, pushed down a rush of nausea that rolled through her, and turned. Nothing happened. She leaned into the door, and twisted the knob a little more. Still nothing.

"This can't be right. You're supposed to be the key. The one who can open the door." Elech growled and paced behind her. "Try again," he demanded.

She studied the door and released the knob. What was wrong? How hard could it be to open a damn door?

Tap into the magic within you, Delila's voice insisted. *It runs through your veins, same as it does mine. Find it within yourself and hold on. It'll give you exactly what you need to do this.*

Daphne nodded, squared her shoulders, and closed her eyes. She focused on every little sensation running through her. Every prickle of instinct. Every rumble of comprehension. Every swell of power. *Ahh.* There it was. She breathed deep, letting the power eclipse everything else within. It sparked, fast and hot, growing to a pinnacle. She opened her eyes and faced the doors once more. This time, she let the power control her. Delila's voice muted by it. Her movements commanded by it. Her every thought, guided by it. Instead of reaching toward the door on the right, her hand went straight to the door on the left.

"What are you doing?"

Even Elech couldn't break through whatever was happening to her.

"You said I'm the key, right?" She swung on him, a scowl pulling on her skin as she waited for his agreement. A silent nod was all he offered.

"Then let me work," she said, her harsh tone rivaling even his worst.

She turned back to the door, gathered the loose ends of her magic into one big collective, and reached for the knob. This time, it turned beneath her hand with ease and a gasp of air from whatever lay beyond seeped out.

"Move," Elech demanded. "I've waited so long for this moment." He turned back to his father and offered him a last glance. "Father, I was honored to deliver the Overworld to you, but it's obvious your loyalties lie elsewhere."

Daphne whimpered when Elech grabbed an arm.

"You will lead us through in case my parents have planned something vile."

Behind them, Daphne heard Delila race into the room, straight for Dema. Daphne paused to see that under Delila's power, the dagger easily withdrew from Dema's chest. Delila helped him to his feet and tucked the bloodied dagger beneath her skirt.

Dema leaned heavily on Delila. "The key will deliver you rightly, my son." He flashed Daphne a small smile and a wink as his tail flicked against the ground. "Get ready to embrace your birthright."

Together, she and Elech moved in tandem toward the door. Daphne stepped ahead of the devil to enter first as planned. But instead of seeing Nephillium as promised, a searing sensation ripped across her skin. She jerked out from under the grip of her devilish escort and fell to the ground. The warm brick beneath her hands and knees soothed the ache as another sharp pain sliced through her shoulders, as if the skin on her back was splitting in half.

Her breath froze in her lungs, her heart moved securely into double time, and her spine arched all in the span of the seconds it took for her to realize her mistake. She had listened to her magic and it had steered her wrong. This wasn't the Overworld. There wasn't anyone here to save her. There wasn't an army of angels poised beyond her sight, with magical arrows aimed at the monster beside her. *No*.

Her body revolted. A scream ripped from her chest. The searing pain took hold and stopped all flow of rational thought. A gasp from somewhere registered, but she couldn't focus on it. Her clothes were too tight. She needed them gone. Now. Her fingers grappled with her shirt, but couldn't find a hold. Tears rolled down her face and the fabric pulled tight as the strain of her body stretched it beyond its capacity to conform.

The welcome hiss of fabric tearing hit her ears and release followed. She crouched into herself her spine arced, elongated, and stretched as if a cat's from her head to the tip of a tail. A tail that flicked from side to side, looking for balance as she screamed and shook with the shock of it all. This couldn't be happening. She searched her mind for Delila, but only found silence. For once in the last twenty-four hours, she would give anything to hear the witch in her head, telling her what the hell was happening.

"Oh my God. Daphne?"

Nic's quiet voice laced with confusion and she was certain if she could bring herself to look at him, she'd see the same confusion clearly etched across his features. The pain shot from the center of her being until nothing else mattered. Not Nic. Not Elech. Not Dema. Not even Delila. Only the pain mattered. A swell of heat surrounded her like little fingers of flame touching her body, soothing her sore spots until the pain dulled into submission.

"Dema, this isn't right. Something's gone horribly wrong."

Delila's voice wasn't right. It was loud and full and sounded nothing like it had in her head, Daphne realized. She looked over her shoulder, searching for the source of it and was stunned to find a full set of wings protruding from her skin. Big, black, feather covered wings. They fluttered as her mind willed it, then stretched to their full span as if to prove they belonged to her. She shook her head and begged her mind to stop playing this trick on her, and was tickled on her leg by none other than a tail. And not just any tail. But her tail. *Shit.*

"Dema, we have to do something." Delila's voice carried to her.

"I'm not sure there is anything to be done. It's her fate." The devil king fell to the ground, his hand clutched to his side.

"How'd this happen? How was she able to open the door to the Underworld? The prophecy said she would be the key to getting us into the Overworld," Elech screeched.

Elech's whine was enough to send Daphne into a rage. How dare he? He was the reason this was happening to her. He was the reason she was here. It was all his fault. He forced her into becoming this… this… this monster. She rose to her feet, oblivious to the fact that her clothes were completely gone and left her bare. She needed him to shut up.

"Mother?" Elech's voice rose an octave. "Impossible. You're dead."

Daphne whirled around to face the beast who'd done this to her. "More impossible than this?" She gestured to her body as her wings spread out behind her and her tail snaked up around her leg and rested at her knee. "What've you done to me?"

FOURTEEN

DAPHNE

NO ONE SPOKE. Sulfur scented air swirled around them and blistering heat scorched the landscape. The Underworld met all the hellish expectations Daphne had. She waited for fear to take hold as she stood before her posse in all her devilish glory. This couldn't be right. There was no way she was a devil, too. She couldn't be.

Daphne surveyed the faces of the people she loved and cringed. This wasn't a bad dream. A hallucination. A mistake. She was a monster. Of all the looks, Colin's hurt the most. Horror. Denial. More horror.

The man who'd told her he wanted her only a few hours ago, now refused to meet her eyes and shrunk away from what she'd become. *Dammit all to hell.* The irony of it all sent a ripple of laughter to her lips.

"What. Have. You. Done?" Menace dripped from every syllable Elech spoke as he approached her. "This isn't the Overworld."

"Do you really think, I wanted to wind up here? That I planned to land myself in the Underworld? Like this?" Daphne stared him down and her tail slashed through the air, prepared for the chance to fight. "You are the one who brought me here to choose. You were the one who told me to open the door that felt 'right.' You were the one who saw the other door refuse to open for me. So, what makes you think I had anything to do with this?"

Elech's hand shot toward her and she braced for the impact, but it never came. Instead, his long fingers wrapped around the tender skin of her throat.

"You little bitch," he spat, his breath hot on her face. "You can't tell me you aren't responsible for all of this." He pointed to the visage of his mother. "For her."

Daphne studied the woman who had spent most of the last hours buried deep inside of her mind and was surprised at how much she resembled Callie. Although, Callie was fully human and still safe and sound at the Dews. This woman was older, and not quite so...solid? Delila's form wavered as if one with the heat of the place to prove her point. *Interesting*.

The hand at her throat tightened. "Take me into the Overworld," Elech seethed.

Her hands fought against his grip, aimed at prying his fingers from her skin, while her legs flailed and her wings beat against his in what could only look like two big ass birds of prey fighting.

Tears stung her eyes as she struggled for breath. It wasn't going to end like this. She couldn't let it end like this. She had to fight.

Through her tears, she witnessed two things her brain refused to comprehend; Colin holding Nic from coming to her aid, and Dema and Delila cowered together as if the scene playing out before them was nothing more than a stage play. Nic jabbed at the shifter's face with a swift uppercut and threw himself onto Elech's back, pummeling the devil with his fists. As ineffective as she thought his assault was, it was enough to get Elech to loosen his hold on her throat.

"Leave my sister alone." Nic's harsh words hit her ears and offered her the reprieve she needed.

Her wings beat behind her, lifting her off the ground until Elech could no longer reach her.

"Run!" She yelled toward the others. "Go back through. Leave me here. Seal the door." As the words flew from her mouth, their impact hit her full force. This was it. The moment her entire life had been leading up to. She was going to die with the devil. Better yet, she was going to die as a devil.

Colin grabbed Dema, anchored him to his side and together they moved toward the door. She readied herself to dive for Elech, but Delila's shimmery form caught her eye. She mouthed something. Back? Blood? What the hell was she trying to say? The ghostly woman made a slashing motion with her hand and mouthed the word again. *Oh. Blade.* Fate's blade to be exact. The only blade that could wound the devil and remove his powers. The blade he'd used on too many of her loved ones. The blade strapped to the witch's thigh beneath her long skirt.

Elech pounded a fist into Nic's core and he doubled over. The moment he paused between blows was her chance. Shaky and insecure about her wings' ability to guide her, she dove toward Delila and hoped for the best. Learning how to fly mid battle wasn't smart. Forget smart. It wasn't sane. She crashed into the devil and her brother with the grace of a duck mid hunting season, and they collapsed on the ground in a tangle of limbs.

"Nic. Run." She ground out between her teeth as Elech's fingers scraped her skin, tearing to get to her. "Now!"

"No."

Sweet, stoic Nic. Never made a fuss. Never rocked the boat. Never pushed for anything. Until now. Damn him. Why couldn't he just keep on being his usual agreeable self. But, no. That would be too damn easy.

"There's no reason for both of us to die," she argued and aimed a fist toward Elech's face.

"Who said dying was the only option?" Nic grunted as Elech's foot connected with his shin.

"I did," Elech seethed. "You two are useless. I needed the key to the Overworld and got the key to the Underworld. As far as I'm concerned, death is your best option."

Elech avoided her fist with seconds to spare, but managed to grab chunk of her hair and pulled. Hard. Venom spiked through her bloodstream.

Only bitches pulled hair and she was tired of him being a bitch. As if conjured by her thoughts, her fingernails elongated into claws. Claws would work. This time, she flailed her fingers out to their fullest and swiped at Elech's face. If she could draw enough blood to distract him, she stood a chance to get the blade from Delila.

Her bad luck held when Nic's face appeared in front of her claws, where mere seconds ago Elech's had been. Time slowed until she was aware of every microsecond. The beat of her heart. The sweat rolling down her skin. The pluck of a feather dislodged from her brand new wings. The adrenaline spike when her claws made contact with Nic's skin. Panic shot through her faster than a bullet train without brakes and her claws retracted, but not before a single, long, bloodied gash appeared on Nic's face. *Shit.*

When time returned to normal, three things happened that would forever change her world: Nic's distraction resulted in his body crumpling to the floor like a wet rag doll, lifeless. Delila threw the dagger toward her, and Elech intercepted the throw, plunging the blade deep into her unprotected abdomen.

Daphne wasn't sure why, but dying on the brick road leading into the heart of the Underworld felt like the final stanza of the poetry that was her life. She clutched the handle of the blade and her wings surrounded her in a protective embrace.

Leave it in or pull it out?
Leave it in or pull it out?

111

Leave it in or pull it out?

The question ran through her head on repeat while her brain grasped for years old first aid training. Laying on the floor beside her was Nic. His eyes were fixed and unfocused. If she was going to die, at least she wouldn't be alone. She entered this life with him and she'd be content to follow him out of it.

Don't give up. Dema and your love are working on a plan. Wafted through her head.

Unable to focus on the wavering image of Delila, she focused on Elech. From the buildings surrounding them came demons, lost souls, creatures she didn't have a name for. They surrounded them and bowed low before the devil, waiting for his command.

"Finish them."

Two words. That was all it would require to end her.

As the creatures began to surround them, she slid herself over Nic's body even if only to save him from any further torment. A crash exploded in her ears and the heat of the sidewalk welcomed her skin.

"Stop."

Dema? He was back? Hadn't he been too weak to fight? She raised her head to find the source of the voice and landed on the king of the Underworld's silver eyes. Wait. Silver? *Holy moly.* She was in trouble. Laying on the floor, surrounded by a pool of her own blood and her heart raced at the sight of Colin in all his cool shape-shifted-demon-king-lookalike-glory. It was a good thing she would die from the blade so death by embarrassment wasn't an option.

Daphne took the moment of distraction to yank the blade from her body. She sprang to her feet in a coordinated effort with her wings and lunged at the devil. The look on Elech's face would forever be etched in her memory. Clinging to the blade, she soared over his head and made two strong, decisive, instinctual swipes with the blade. Each one landing in perfect time to catch the base of his wings. If nothing else, the devil would officially be grounded. Forever. She tucked her tail between her legs and curled her body against the oncoming impact of the floor. She was done for. It was over. Someone else would have to take up the fight. Her effectiveness was toast. The wound in her side burned and the heat of the sidewalk prickled her skin. She waited for his retaliation, but it never came.

Elech rose to his full height and screamed. Howled. Roared. But before he could make a move, Colin gestured toward the devil and commanded, "Take him." As if a switch had been flipped, the horde of hell haunts turned on Elech and grabbed at him until he was restrained under their collective strength, his wings on the floor, bloodied behind him.

Delila raced to her side and gently touched her wounded abdomen. With a cluck, she pried the handle of the dagger from Daphne's hand and tucked it beneath her skirt.

113

"Move slowly. Back in the apothecary I'm sure I have a salve to help with that." Delila helped her to her feet and felt solid beneath her as she pressed her weight into her ancestor's side.

"What about Nic? We can't leave him. Not here," Daphne sobbed.

"Of course not. He'll need his body once he figures out how to get back in." Delila ushered her forward, over the threshold into the apothecary.

Beyond the doorway she could see the outline of Nephillium huddled over Dema. Both looked so different and yet similar almost as if they were the opposite faces of the same being.

"Get back in?" Delila's words took a minute to take root in her head. "What do you mean?"

"It appears both of you had some dormant traits. What I don't understand is how the prophecy was so wrong. With Nic's ability to spirit shift, he must be fated to hold a post after his earthly life. And you... Well, I don't know what exactly to make of you." Delila shook her head and led her to Dema. "Here. Sit. I'll see what I can find for your wound." She helped Daphne to the ground.

"We might need the help of the other witches," Nephillium whispered once Delila joined him by a huge shelf full of vials, but not quiet enough that Daphne couldn't hear him. "Fate's blade isn't known for allowing its victims to live."

Daphne lowered herself fully to the ground beside the real Dema, so their heads were merely inches apart.

"What was Colin thinking going in there as you? Better yet, how could you let him do it?" She stared into the depths of his soul and hoped she could read any deception he might offer.

"That man will do anything for you. I'm surprised he's been able to focus, considering your current state." Dema pointed a finger at the wound in her gut. "Hurts like a demon doesn't it?"

"You should know," she retorted and would've laughed had it not hurt so damn bad. For the first time since sprouting wings and a tail, she took a good look at the length of her own body. "How do you put up with this damn tail?"

Incredulity was Dema's only response.

"Oh, sweet Daphne. You'll see that having a tail has its advantages," Nephillium chimed in with a wink as one uncoiled from beneath the base of his wings in silent solidarity. "You do realize it's the natural form of born Guardians. Unlike humans we don't change our form to hide what makes us special."

"That doesn't mean I plan on walking around like this for the rest of my life." It occurred to her that she might not have much of a choice in the matter as blood still poured from the open gash in her gut.

"Lie still," Delila ordered and pressed a paste to her wound.

The smell of cinnamon and cloves mixed with a hint of something sweet wafted to her nose. "What is that?" She reached a hand toward her wound.

"Leave it be. This mixture should slow the bleeding and clean the cut." Concern creased Delila's brow despite her upbeat tone. Then she leaned over Dema, pressed a kiss to his lips and whispered something Daphne couldn't hear.

Daphne watched Delila rise to her feet and move toward the dual doors. With no effort at all she opened the one leading to the Underworld and crossed the threshold.

"What is she doing?"

"Ensuring Elech's imprisonment."

"But I thought that's what Colin was there for." She winced as she tried to sit upright. Her tail tapped on the ground as if annoyed she'd been so careless with their body.

"Ah, he is, but his disguise will only get him so far."

She let his words worm their way into the part of her brain still working. Her heartbeat kicked into high gear at the implication. *Shit.* Colin had been in there all alone while she'd been doing what? Laying here, feeling sorry for herself? The man she'd only known for such a short time who'd offered her so much to keep her safe and how would she repay him? By letting him give it all to protect her. She struggled to her feet and when her legs threatened to fail, her wings beat on their own giving her the slight edge of flight to move her forward. There was no stopping. Not now. Not until she knew Colin was safe and Nic's body could be recovered.

"Don't be foolish."

She ignored Nephillium and continued forward, her slow pace agonizing as scenarios of torment and death flashed through her mind. She pushed forward and grasped the doorknob with all her might. Before she could turn the knob, the door flew open and sent her off balance. She pitched forward and landed in the arms of none other than Colin. Not a single word formed in her brain, but tears of relief flowed like dual rivers down her cheeks. She grabbed him hard and refused to let go.

"It's okay," he soothed. "It's okay."

She shook her head and ran her hands over his flesh before extending them to his shifted wings, needing to ensure he was unharmed and whole.

"I'm okay, Daph. But you need to sit. You're bleeding." With that he gathered her in his arms and cradled her demon form to his own. "Where's Callie? She might be able to help. I've seen her work some pretty incredible magic in the last twenty-four hours."

"Last I saw her; she was back at the Dews." She nodded her head toward the entrance to the apothecary room. "But I need to get Nic out of there." She attempted to wiggle out of his embrace, but he held her even tighter.

"I can't let you go back in there. Understand?" He gave her a warning glare and set his mouth in a grimace.

"But…"

"But nothing. You stay here and rest and I'll go get him." He paused and an odd look washed over his devilish face, clouding his silver eyes. "You do know he didn't make it, right?" He braced her against his chest and tucked her head beneath his chin. "I'm sorry we couldn't save him." His tail entwined with hers and it shot a ripple of yearning through her.

Hot liquid heat scorched a path through her body, igniting nerve endings she forgot she had until it pooled in her center, burning against the salve in her wound as if sealing it from the inside. A shudder rippled through her and Colin tensed.

"Sorry. The damn thing seems to have a mind of its own," he explained as he laid her gently on the floor.

She watched with awe as every bit of him began to shimmer. Soon the edges of his wings blurred and his face contorted. Unlike the pain she had felt during her transformation, his appeared fluid and natural. The graceful nature of his shifting brought a warmth to her heart. How beautiful would it be to be able to shift into such a monster in one moment and then revert back to her human form. Without the pain. Without the struggle. Without the knowledge that her inner monster was nothing shy of evil. She closed her eyes against the truth of it all and wished she could return to her human form if only to remind Colin she had one. That they really weren't so different. If only he could see her as human once more. Then maybe she stood a chance of finding some sort of normal.

A pang of guilt washed over her. She wasn't normal. She'd never been normal. She'd never stand a chance at a normal life, and surely not with a guy as wonderful as Colin.

"Penny for your thoughts."

She reluctantly opened her eyes, but couldn't bring herself to see the look in his. Instead, she focused on his lips and the trickle of blood seeping down his face from where he'd been cut and wished herself away. "I'm just worried about Nic," she lied. There was no way in hell she would tell the man who'd just risked his life for hers to understand her wanton need to be loved and accepted now that she knew no one would ever see more than the devil within. She shook her head and rolled up to a sitting position. She tried to cover as much of her nakedness as she could. As if acting on instinct alone, her wings folded across her body, cocooning her in an embrace.

"I'll see if it's clear. Delila said she had someone in there who could help. But she told me it'd be best if I didn't stick around for that." He knelt before her in all his humanness. "Please don't be sad. He fought hard to save you. Your brother would've been glad to see you on this side of it."

Behind them, Callie rushed into the room.

"Daphne! Ohmygod, are you okay?" Callie stopped short and cocked her head. "Shit. What the hell happened to you?" She pointed to Daphne's tail which was wavering along the floor where it had previously been intertwined with Colin's. "Did Thirteen do that?"

"Nope. Turns out I wasn't the key to the Overworld after all. I was more destined for the

Underworld." She dropped her eyes to her tail and could commiserate with its sad demeanor.

"Oh, no."

Callie's hands on her wings weighed her down even more. "Nothing I can do about it though. And to make things worse, Nic somehow got separated from his body." She raised her eyes toward the doorway to the Underworld. "Colin offered to go get his body, but I'm not sure where Nic's spirit is."

Callie waved a 'shhh' then looked at a point above their heads.

"Nic is freaking out. He can't figure out how to get back in his body," Callie relayed. "But he's glad you're okay. Although he seemed a little worried about all that," she gestured at Daphne's body. "Said something about he always knew you were a brat, but never thought you were a damn devil."

"Is he all right?" Daphne looked to the place where Callie was staring, but saw nothing. "How can you hear him? Is he a ghost like Delila was?"

"He looks like himself, so I'm sure he's fine... Shhh, I'm not talking to you, Nic," she chastised before turning back to Daphne. "I think I am able to communicate with anyone walking on this plane in their spirit form. Nic's 'ghosting' and I can communicate with him. He must have some sort of gift. Although, makes sense considering you guys have a witch and devil among your ancestors."

"Ghosting? Does that mean he won't be able to get back into his body?"

Callie shrugged. "I wouldn't think so. It's not like he's actually dead. More like he stepped out of his body for a bit." She nodded at something and agreed, "Yeah, I know it's frustrating, but I'm sure we'll figure out how to get you back in there in no time."

Nephillium, who had been tending Dema, rose to his feet and looked at where Daphne assumed Nic wafted. "Spirit shifting can be an indicator of a Guardian. Most don't actually experience it until they pass from human existence into the Overworld, but I've never seen a human shift into a Guardian's form before today either and your young suitor did just that."

"He's not my suitor," Daphne protested as she probed the wound in her stomach.

"Who? Colin? You could do far worse than him. He's a hunk," chimed in Callie.

"Hey! I'm right here" grumped Jason as he struggled to his feet, rubbing his throat.

"Yes you are," Callie cooed and wrapped herself in his arms.

For a few blissful seconds it was almost easy to forget nothing would ever be the same in her life again.

"You do realize, your wound has begun to heal ever since his tail mated with yours," Nephillium interjected. "I'm pretty sure that means you're soul mates."

Before she could bask in the glow of the Guardian's declaration, Colin crossed back over into the apothecary with Nic in his arms. Both had slices across their faces. Nic's wasn't nearly as deep as Colin's, but both were crusted over with dried blood.

"Lay him here," Callie commanded and pointed to a spot beside Daphne. "And maybe you should go get some clothes. For you and Daph," she added.

"Yeah. Pretty sure mine are back at the Dews, but hers…" He paused and passed the briefest of glances over her still devilish form. "Hers got destroyed in there when she shifted."

"Run upstairs to my apartment. Something in my closet will fit her."

"Even with the wings and stuff?"

This time Colin didn't even bother to look her way. He spoke to Callie as if she wasn't there and couldn't hear the disgust in his voice. So much for being soul mates.

"Yes. Get something baggy," Callie ordered, her irritation hard to disguise.

Daphne watched the man she'd come to trust walk away without looking back. Damn. It hurt. His rejection. Her self-esteem. The slice in her midsection. Ugh. At the thought of her injury, a sizzling, burning pain erupted beneath her fingertips. She released the pressure she'd been holding and watched her skin stitch itself back together as if by magic. Surely, Nephillium was mistaken. Delila had used the same concoction on Dema and she had touched him plenty since he'd been injured, although it appeared his time was nearing an end. But now that she thought about it,

Colin had been wounded by the blade too and he appeared to be healing as well.

Delila burst through the doorway and raced to Dema's side. "Aaró has Elech. He's ensured he will keep him under lock and key. Now, how can I help you, my darling?"

"Fate's blade is notorious for its destructive powers," Nephillium answered. "Maybe it needs to be destroyed."

Daphne studied the scene before her. Delila was so engrossed in Dema she didn't seem aware of the Guardian's motives, which appeared anything other than pure with the glint in his eye.

"I have an idea." Delila sprang to her feet, withdrew the blade from beneath the folds of her skirt and pressed a kiss to Dema's pale lips. Without another word, she strode from the room, head held high.

She returned minutes later empty handed. Whatever she had done, it must have destroyed the blade, because the wound in Daphne's side had even stopped aching and Dema looked like a man on the mend.

"Darling, what've you done?" His razor sharp tone cut through the air.

"What needed to be done." She wiped her hands together as if to remove any residual energy remaining on her skin after touching the artifact. "Now, Elech will never again be able to hurt those I love. Although…" She turned to Nephillium and glared, "I don't think the flame is up for the task of disposing of the scrolls any longer."

Daphne tried to understand the veiled meaning behind her ancestor's words, but was at a loss.

"You didn't," the Guardian spat.

"I did," Delila assured.

"Stupid woman."

With those last words the Guardian, disappeared from the room in the blink of an eye.

"How do you feel, darling?" Delila dropped beside Daphne and ran a hand through her hair. "Has your wound healed?"

Daphne removed her hand and exposed her skin to the witch. "I think I'm as good as I can be all things considered."

"Why do you sound so sad?"

"Well, I'm a devil now, so there goes my chances at a normal life. My haunted B&B can now be renamed the Hell Hotel and I can be the main attraction." Tears ran freely down her cheeks.

"You do realize this form is nothing more than a manifestation of your true self, right?" The concern in Delila's face was almost too much to manage. "As much as I could take on the form of the crone, you can take on the form of the devil. It will only take a bit of practice to learn how to make the choice for yourself."

"But even if I do learn how to go back to normal, seeing me like this," she waved her hands over her winged self, "isn't something someone could easily forget."

A slight pull of Delila's lips suggested otherwise. "If we're talking about who I think we are, I have it on good authority that time will make this easier to accept for all involved."

Was that a wink? Delila had lost her damn mind if she truly thought there was still a chance for her and Colin. Speak of the devil and he shall appear. He wore a pair of jeans that hugged his powerful frame and his unbuttoned shirt made her long for him to look at her with those sweet bedroom eyes once again. But, he could barely glance her way as he passed her a pair of sweatpants and a tank top.

"I figured this might work with your wings," he offered, without making eye contact.

"Thanks."

"Yeah. Sure." He shuffled his feet.

"Why don't you help Dema into the other room," Delila suggested. "I'll join him in a second and then you and Daphne should get back to the Dews. Now that Elech has been dealt with, it's time for life to start moving forward again." She paused, and smiled at Daphne. "Besides, I've been told you have someone who had been waiting a long time to see you." Delila winked.

"Mom?"

Delila nodded and Daphne dropped the clothes to the floor and flung her arms around the witch. "Thank you," she sobbed.

"Darling, you did this all on your own. Although, good luck explaining Nic."

"Well, I can help translate for him until he can figure out how to get back in his body," chimed in Callie.

125

The thought of seeing her mother for the first time in years looking like this monster was enough to make her sick to her stomach. Never would she allow the woman who had given her soul to save her see her looking as evil as the devil who had tormented them. She closed her eyes and shuddered at the thought. With all her focus on forbidding her mother from seeing her in this state, a burning began behind her shoulder blades.

A spasm shot across her back and plucked at the nerve endings of her spinal column. Pain exploded behind her eyes. *Not again.* She dropped to the floor and curled in a ball. This couldn't be happening.

"Daphne!"

Her name was a cry on Colin's lips from across the room, but she couldn't bring herself to raise her head and meet his surely horrified stare. Whatever was happening must be worse than her transformation into her devilish self. And she refused to replace even the small sliver of remaining hope that he'd be able to remember her as she had been with what surely was the most abject horror she could even imagine. She embraced the pain streaming through her body and gave herself over to it until sweet oblivion took hold.

FIFTEEN

DAPHNE

DAPHNE AWOKE, CLOTHED, and human in her childhood bed. Never had she imagined the easiest thing she'd do today would be send the Jersey Devil to the Underworld for the rest of forever, but as her eyes landed on Colin, she knew it was true. She tucked the inkling of hope that bubbled up upon seeing him sitting across the room away and focused on her mom, sitting vigil beside her. How many times had she been in that same spot in the long term care facility over the years, holding her mother's hand, willing her to wake up?

"Baby girl," Hope cooed, her voice the most magical sound Daphne had ever heard.

"Mom. You're back." She sat up and embraced her with the strength of a thousand hellhounds. The thought of letting go, never even entered her head.

"We've been worried about you," Hope choked out around her tears.

"Um, I think I'll head downstairs," Colin offered and practically sprinted for the door.

"That young man has been worried sick about you," Hope whispered. "He carried you here, tucked you in, and refused to leave. He must be someone very special."

"Oh, mom. I wish you were right. I think he just feels obligated. He'd been sent to help us and there was a little body snatching mishap that sorta confused things between us." Daphne loosened her arms and looked her mom in the eyes. "My word, it is damn nice to see you up and about. I thought I'd never get to talk to you like this again."

"My sweet girl, this is a dream come true. Your father. You. Nic."

Her mom's empty pause where Dax's name should've been haunted her. "I'm sorry about Dax, mom." A fresh well of tears sprang forth in her eyes.

"I know you are. I'm just glad I'm not here mourning all three of you." She smiled and tucked a strand of hair behind Daphne's ear. "Your brother wouldn't want to see you this way. What's done is done and a piece of Dax will always live on in each of our hearts," she soothed. Hope's face brightened with a forced smile, "Come now, let's go get you something to eat. You look too skinny for a full grown woman."

Laughter ticked in her chest. "Yes, mom."

Hand in hand, they joined the rest of the family in the dining room.

"She's awake," Callie called and rushed to wrap her in a bear hug.

"That's what they tell me," Daphne replied with a wink.

"Well, Delila insisted that you would awake soon and we all be here when you do."

She scanned the room. Jason. Dad. Nic's body settled in a chair looking as lifeless as it had before. "Why?"

"You know Delila, she's not one to give a lot of information."

"So Nic hasn't, um, gotten back in yet?" She nodded toward her brother.

"Nope. He says it's not as easy as losing your wings and tail. But he's also pretty hungry so if there's anything that will motivate your brother back into his body, it might be your dad's famous lasagna." Callie raised her eyebrow as if listening to something, then shook her head. "Your sister isn't going to agree to that. She finally got her old body back. She's not going to give it up in a show of solidarity, buddy."

"No. She sure as hell isn't."

Colin's abrupt answer startled her. The silver of his eyes turned dark and stormy gray.

"He was joking," Callie chided. "No one wants Daphne to go full demon on us."

"Least of all me," Daphne added and dropped her gaze to the floor.

"Let's eat." Her dad had spent so many years depressed, searching for the solution to reunite his family, and now he sounded positively giddy.

Daphne smiled and pulled out a chair. Just for tonight she would be normal. She would relish this last day of fitting in and pretend there wasn't something horribly wrong living deep inside. Everyone took their seats and she took a beat to memorize every angle of their collective faces. She was surrounded by all the people she loved in the world. Loved more than life itself. Hell, only hours ago she'd been willing to say goodbye to each and every one of them if it meant saving them from Elech's evil plans. Each one of them held an important hunk of her heart in their hands.

A hunk they might not cherish as much as she hoped they would, her brain challenged when her eyes landed on Colin. After all they'd been through, there was no way she could imagine her life without him in it, but he was hard to read. His eyes the color of steel and as hard to penetrate as the metal, she was losing hope. He'd seemed weary ever since the battle in Hell. Whether from the experience itself, or having seen her contort into a devil, complete with wings and a damn tail, she wasn't sure.

She ran her gaze over his expansive chest and wondered if he'd stiffen beneath her hand if she touched him. He shifted in his seat as if her thoughts had permeated his mind and set off a recoil. What was she thinking? She closed her eyes and tried to focus on Jason. He and Callie sat side by side. With every slight movement either of them made, there was a constant point of contact between them as if they were tied together by unseen forces.

Jason rambled on and on about something and gestured to a decanter sitting front and center on table. Small shot glasses surrounded the crystal and beckoned to her. She tried to focus on Jason's words, but they didn't register. All her brain could conjure was an image of her, grabbing Colin, planting a kiss on his lips, and begging him to forget everything, pleading with him to remember she wasn't a monster.

Her heart stumbled and her stomach dropped. She *was* a monster; the dull ache between her shoulder blades a less than subtle reminder. Even if she begged him to give her another chance, she would never forget the horror-filled look on his face when he had seen her take the devilish form of her ancestor. Disgust, pure and simple. There was no unseeing it. Not for her. Not ever.

"Look, it's not as simple as waking up with a clean slate."

Jason's reprimand jostled her back to the present.

"It's an option to help move beyond," Jason intoned. "Think of it as a way to make the most impactful thing in your brain get erased. We used it on Dax's girlfriend and I'm almost positive she won't remember him."

"Which will be a blessing for her, all things considered," Callie added and wound herself deeper into Jason's side as if he was the source of her energy.

"So this will take away the memories we have of Thirteen?"

131

Her dad's whispered question brought her fully into the conversation. "You can't seriously be considering this? Are you?" Anger bubbled up and threatened to spill out. A prickle of sensation played over her spine and she fought the press of her bonus extremities beneath the surface of her skin, ready to burst through with a wicked vengeance as her ire rose. "You can't think this is a good idea. Tell him. It's insane." She turned eyes on her mother and waited for her to jump into the fight, but the haunted look in Hope's eyes hurt. "Forgetting things set all this into motion," Daphne insisted. "Mom?"

"You might be right, sweetheart, but wouldn't it be nice to be able to live without knowing you're a skeleton key to the Underworld?"

Ouch. If Colin had been on the fence about the prospect of downing the *Forget* potion, she could see the shift in his thinking written all over his handsome face when he reached across the table and fingered the rim of a shot glass.

"I've seen what this potion can do," Colin admitted as he slid the glass in front of him.

"You have?" Confusion warred with suspicion. She knew he had secrets, but this sucked.

"A good friend's husband took it when he thought he had no other choice and it saved them a lot of heartache." He reached back into the center of the table, uncorked the decanter, and poured the clear liquid into his glass. He paused with the open container mid-air and looked her right in the face for the first time since returning from the

Underworld. "If you could rewind time, would you? Go back. Before the pain. The knowing. The heartache. Now imagine living your life from here on out as if you were starting there." His grey eyes shone silver in the crystalline light hanging over the table.

He wasn't wrong. There was a part of her that would give anything to go back to a time when she didn't know she was anything other than a woman living a normal life. A woman who couldn't transform into a flying beast. A woman who could wield a small dagger with such deadly force. A woman whose body wanted the one man who struggled to meet her eyes. This was her chance. She could start over. Start fresh. And if she could keep her anger under control, maybe she'd never need to know about the devilish nature beneath the surface of her consciousness.

A nod was all it took. Plain. Elegant. Simple. Colin poured another dose, corked the decanter, and slid the glass in front of her.

"Here's to a fresh start." He lifted his glass in mock salute.

Daphne lifted hers in kind and willed her hand still. Another nod, a clink of glass on glass, and a tip of the head was all it took to make the biggest mistake of her life. One that registered only as the last of the liquid slipped effortlessly down her throat. Colin stood, circled the table, and swung his heavy arms around her in a bear hug. The smell of his skin drifted through the fabric of his tee and wrapped around the sensory receptors in her brain without sticking. The low rumble of his deep voice slithered down her spine as the heat of his breath tickled her ear.

"Under different circumstances, you'd've been all mine. Fuck Fate."

A long blink later, and she found herself alone and tucked beneath a blanket on the plush cushions of the couch. When had she laid down? Was she home? Was mom stroking her hair? Questions roared at her, each one demanding to be answered before the last.

"Mom?"

"Hey, baby girl. How are you feeling?" Concern creased her brow and Nic came to peer over their mother's shoulder with a broad smile on his face.

Daphne rolled her shoulders and wiggled to a seated position. The space between her shoulder blades burned. *Oh, no you don't* she wordlessly chided the wings hidden beneath her skin. The wings? *Oh shit.* Jason must've messed up the potion, because the events of the last day assaulted her with the clarity of lightening in a glass sphere.

"She awake?"

"Cal, I think the spell didn't work. I remember everything," she insisted as her friend settled beside her on the sofa.

"I'm sorry, sweetie," Callie soothed and ran a hand in circles across her back. "We can always try again."

"Maybe it's better this way..." She wrapped her hands together in her lap and looked between her mom and her best friend. "I can't help but think I dodged a bullet."

The front door opened and her dad and Jason strode through, fatigue clinging to the features.

"How'd it go?" An eyebrow arched on Callie's face as she propelled herself off the couch and into Jason's waiting arms.

"Good, but it took the both of us to drag his ass into the house. Almost left him in the car and walked home." He shook his head and ruffled Callie's curls. "How are things here?"

Daphne watched the exchange between them with curiosity. What was he talking about? Hadn't Jason and her dad stepped outside for fresh air only moments ago? A look flew between Callie and Jason, unreadable, intimate, and oh so ominous.

And the truth of the matter crashed into her. There was something she didn't know.

The potion had worked.

Damn.

SIXTEEN

DELILA

THE DOOR TO the Underworld closed behind Delila with a finality that echoed in the small apothecary. Her hands shook on their own accord and the empty place in her chest where a human heart would reside, pitched in stilted bursts.

"It was what needed to be done." Dema's tender voice was accompanied by gentle hands. "He won't suffer. At least not for long." A low chuckle rumbled in his chest. "Knowing our son, even without his wings, he'll find a way to rule."

She nodded and snuggled into him. If even an ounce of his strength could rub off on her, she might be able to walk away from this without regrets, but this was more than she could manage.

"It's time."

Somehow she hadn't noticed Nephillium's appearance in the room. The door to the Overworld was open and she could smell the crisp air laced with... Was that sugar cookies? As the Guardian stepped farther into the room, she realized the smell was him.

"I need more time," Dema snarled and pulled her closer into his embrace, surrounding her with both his arms and wings. "As you've pointed out, her choice has been made and this will be the last time I can hold her."

"About that…" the Guardian hedged, "I have a proposition for you." He turned toward Delila and met her eyes with his. "For all you've done, I can allow you a second chance." He flicked his wrist and the door to the Overworld closed and appeared again beside the one leading to the Underworld. "You chose the Underworld before and it's the reason Drammelech will no longer be able to wreak havoc, but the choice left you unable to see your love." He pointed toward Dema and shook his head. "I still don't understand the appeal my brother offers, but I've never seen a more perfect union. Therefore, this is my gift to you. You will have the choice to make again."

"Thank you, my brother," Dema said and hugged her tight.

Nephillium smiled and it glowed like the sun in the small room. She knew he expected her to feel grateful, and she did, but a piece of her hated knowing her son would never set eyes on someone who cared for him for all eternity. A quick glance at Dema told her what she already knew—he also expected her to extend her gratitude to this man.

"Yes, thank you. I appreciate the opportunity," she added.

"Good. Now that's been taken care of, there's one more thing I needed to speak with Delila about." A measured look landed on Dema and his instantaneous response bothered her.

"I see." Dema stepped away and strode to the door. He turned back to her before reaching for the knob and tossed a casual, "Until later" over his shoulder with a wink.

Delila stood in silence as she watched her lover's tail swish behind him in eager anticipation of the later he promised. The door closed behind him with an airless click. Without Dema's supportive arms, she worried her legs would collapse. With the thought, the stool tucked beneath the apothecary table, slid out in silent invitation. She slumped on it and wrapped her arms around her body in an attempt to ward off the chill in the air between her and the Overworld Angel.

"Whatever it is, why couldn't Dema stay?"

"Because I didn't want him to sway you on this." Nephillium strode to the other side of the table and toyed with the pointed edge of a quill rather than meet her eyes. His strange movements piqued her interest. The Guardian wasn't known for outright deception, and yet all the hallmarks of his hidden devil side screamed at her.

"Dema has no sway over me. By now, I'd think you'd know," she challenged.

"Ahh. But he might if he heard what I have to ask of you." He picked up the quill and dropped it into an inkwell. "I need you to correct what your son has caused. Now."

Dread coursed through her as the weight of his words landed heavy and hard in her gut. He was asking for her to undo everything Elech created when he killed her predecessor. Images flowed through her mind of Daphne, Donovan, and Hope. All of them were products of Elech's wrath. Products of her entanglement with Dema. Products of a future the Overworld didn't want to see come into fruition. She swallowed the lump in her throat down and debated over the words to respond.

"Elech sent a lot of things is the wrong direction with his actions. Members of the magical community have been thrown off their directed and intended life course and others who never should've come into being are… I need you to right those wrongs."

"You mean kill them?"

"We both know the consequences of some unions are unmanageable. What I'm asking is that you assess the risk factors of these unions and act accordingly." He plucked the quill from the dark ink and tapped the excess back into the well before conjuring a parchment beneath the tip. She watched in silence as he scribbled what appeared to be a list on the paper. When finished, he slid it in front of her and sighed. "Start with these. Then go into the records hall and gather any scrolls that have multiple symbols on them. As I'm sure you've now guessed, they represent beings of mixed magical heritages. They will be added to the list and dealt with." He dropped the quill to the table and waved his hand over the parchment as ancient words slipped from his lips. "Once you finish this task, the door to the Overworld will open for you so that you and Dema may reunite, but until then, it's more of a showpiece." He walked to the rear of the room and stopped shy of the door.

"Make your decision carefully, Delila. I won't allow a third chance." He turned the knob and pulled the door open. "And if I were you, I'd hurry with the decision. Demogorgon isn't known for his patience," he crooned with a last look over his shoulder. "No matter how much he desires you."

"But the flame no longer exists," she cried out. "Destroying the blade destroyed the fire," she explained. "You know it to be true."

"Ah. It was true. But Fate's responsibility as the great equalizer cannot be so easily escaped. See for yourself," he challenged with a wink.

And with that, he was gone. The door shut behind him. Solid and unyielding. The parchment before her rustled on an invisible breeze, beckoning. She took a moment, steadied her resolve and folded the paper into fourths before tucking it into her gown. The globe in the antechamber glowed and movement caught her eye. Unable to ignore it, she placed her hands on the outer edge of the orb and peered deep within.

The large bottle of *Forget* she had allowed Jason to take from her apothecary sat front and center on a table; a table surrounded by people whose names were surely on her list. She watched without hearing as the young shifter reached for an empty glass and poured the potion until it reached the brim. He turned toward Daphne and said something Delila couldn't hear before pouring the woman a glass of her own.

She couldn't do it. She couldn't take this potential love away from the woman who had sacrificed as much as she had for the chance at a normal life full of love.

The parchment in her pocket rustled, impossible to ignore. She turned away from the orb and went into the records room. Maybe if she got rid of some of the names on the list, she could talk Nephillium into a compromise. Pulling the square from her pocket, she unfolded the list and read the names. As if her feet were guided by instinct, she moved toward the row she had seen her first time in the room. Her hand reached on impulse to the two scrolls clearly marked with multiple symbols. The third one with the three symbols on its outer wrapping and it vibrated with excited energy in her hand. She unrolled the scroll enough to reconfirm her suspicions. A baby. One with witch, devil, and Elemental blood all coursing through its veins. She tucked the scroll sales away and pulled the one with the golden glow off the shelf. She tucked it beneath her arm and left the chamber. This development solidified everything. She hurried to the orb, her skirt tangling her legs. She needed to stop Daphne. To tell her not to take the potion. To hold onto this man who cared for her.

She laid her hands on the orb and watched with dismay as the two shared a toast then tossed the contents down their throats. Delila's nonexistent heart sank. The paper in her hand flittered. She couldn't do this. Not to Daphne. Not again. She watched as Colin leaned in and placed a kiss on Daphne's lips, his eyes dark and stormy. Daphne faltered and slumped over into the chair. Colin shuddered and Jason came around the table to help steady him.

Delila waved a hand over the orb and sound surrounded her as if she stood beside them in the room.

"Promise me you and Callie will never tell her about me or vice versa," Colin begged.

"You might not be what she forgets," Jason reminded.

"If the ripping in my heart right now means what I think it does, yes I will. She can't ever know about us. It'll hurt her. Promise me." The words were low and slurred as Colin fought for control to keep his eyes open. "You owe me at least this."

"I promise." As the words left the witch's mouth, Colin's legs gave out. "Call Charlie. We're going to need some help getting the big guy home," he called to Callie.

Unable to watch any more, she stepped away from the orb. There had to be something she could do to fix this. Something that didn't require her to kill Daphne's baby—a baby she wouldn't even know about for weeks to come. The insistent rustle of the possessed paper in her pocket filled her with anger. This was too much. Damn Nephillium for asking this much of her. She pounded her fist against her leg and held back a wail. Inspiration struck with the impact of her fist. She tucked the scroll under her arm and strode into the apothecary. A quick look at the glow beneath the door to the Overworld hastened her step.

Delila grabbed a cast iron bowl from one of the shelves and set it in the middle of the table in a wire frame so it would hang suspended over a flame. She pawed through the labeled bottles of liquid on the shelves until she found the palm oil. It would do. A generous pour went into the cauldron and the pesky parchment followed. No sooner had the liquid seeped into the strands of linen of the paper, she struck a match and tossed it into the pot. As the oil caught fire, the paper screamed, sputtering beneath the licks of flame. A rumble sounded from beyond the door to the Overworld and she knew time was running out. This was *her* post. No one was going to dictate how she would do it.

She raced from the room and into the records hall. As promised, Fate's Flame burned bright once again with no trace of the dagger that had so recently destroyed it. Without delay, she hurried to the fire.

Dema would never forgive her. Not this time. Not after how many times she'd betrayed him. The simple fact didn't weigh on her. She unrolled the parchment and read her name, glowing golden at the very top. Who was Nephillium to dictate when she'd pass from this post into the afterlife?

She rerolled the paper and held it to the flicker of the flames until it took hold. She dropped it into the bowl. Her pace quickened as she moved through the viewing room to the apothecary. Her feet stumbled and what bits of her that had become whole seemed to disintegrate beneath her without her control. She crossed the threshold and moved toward the set of doors.

The noise behind the left one grew louder, and every synapse in her head misfired as her hand reached for the knob, demanding she change her course of action. Begging her to stop the nonsense. Pleading with her to think it through once more. She shook it all away, guided by the love she hadn't been able to give to Dema, and the knowledge that this choice would give Daphne and Colin a chance for a future together. The knob burned in her hand, but she refused to let go.

Her body failed her before she could turn the knob and fell to the floor, her soul ripped from its otherworldly flesh.

"How did I know you'd choose to be a martyr given the choice?" Dema's chuckle soothed her senses.

"What are you doing here?" She trailed off as her soulmate reached a hand toward her essence.

"Darling Delila," he hummed. "As a Guardian of the Overworld it is my honor to usher the new souls to their final resting place." He tipped her chin upward and placed a gentle kiss where her lips would be. "I'm so glad you chose me this time, even if it meant ending you."

"How is this possible?"

"In all my years, I've never seen anyone outwit my young brother with such defiant brilliance. Come now, my love. Our forever begins."

He offered his hand and she placed all she could give in it.

"Will I ever have more to offer you?" She hoped her true love could forgive her one last time.

"Trust me, you give me all I ever needed." He led her over the threshold into the Overworld.

With their crossing, her body took shape and her feet touched the ground. All was as it belonged. Daphne was safe. Her baby would live. She and Dema would live happily ever after. And the fate of the supernatural community was now squarely in their own hands.

A content smile slipped across her lips and warmed her from head to toe. She was finally the rebel she always fancied herself to be and it felt amazing.

Epilogue

Drammelech

DRAMMELECH CRAWLED ACROSS the heated bricks on his hands and knees, his tail dragging behind as the screams and sulfur scent of the Underworld assaulted his senses. Condemned to this place. This body. This *hell*. He pounded his hand on the brick beneath him until the skin stung. How dare they banish him? Who did they think they were dealing with?

"Come my Lord," an impish man commanded.

"What do you want with me?" He snarled.

"You are the son of Demogorgon, correct?" The man rose to his tiptoes and glanced nervously over his shoulder.

"I am."

"Good. Then the master prepared a space for you. Follow me," he instructed as he helped Drammelech to his feet then led them deep into a maze of buildings. "Your father knew you'd want all the creature comforts of home," the man explained as they waited by a bank of elevators in the tallest building.

When the elevator landed at their destination, Drammelech was welcomed into a huge gallery full of images of his mother. "Who are you?" He demanded of the man. "And why do you choose to torture me so?"

"I'm Aaró. I've served humbly by the side of every ruler of the Underworld since its inception. Your father asked me to look after you. Said something about knowing you will one day be the most feared and respected leader we've had." He busied himself at a bar tucked against one wall then produced two goblets filled with amber-colored liquid. "A toast?" He suggested and handed one of the glasses to Drammelech.

"To what? My failure?"

"One's failure is another's success," Aaró chided. "What's your first order of business, sir?"

Drammelech took in the room. "Redecorating." He sipped the liquid and tossed the rest on one of the largest paintings.

Aaró nodded and took a deep drink from his glass. "Indeed." He withdrew a small piece of wood from his pocket, flicked the top until a flame appeared and tossed it on the liquor covered painting. "Welcome home, my Lord," he reiterated with a low bow.

For the first time since his internment, Drammelech smiled. Home. It had nice ring to it.

THE END

CAN'T GET ENOUGH?

WANT A SNEAK PEEK AT WHAT'S

COMING NEXT?

Visit www.jeniburns.com for upcoming
announcements and book release information.

BIOGRAPHY

MEET JENI

JENI BURNS is a Jersey Girl through and through, regardless where her mail is delivered. She lives in and is renovating an old Colonial with her husband, two kids, and one massive poodle.

Amidst all the chaos, she squirrels away in her office with her giant cup of decaf, a handful of Swedish Fish, and writes until the natives get restless and drag her back to reality.

FIRE'S REVENGE SNIPPET

IF YOU THOUGHT Elech's evilness could only be contained to one series, you'd be wrong. Take a peek into *Fire's Revenge*, the first novel in the Elemental Love series featuring elementals, witches, and our favorite devil.

FIRE'S REVENGE

ONE
OVERWORLD
CIRCA 1725

Fate knew her job as pseudo-deity was important and she took it as seriously as a being in the Overworld could. That was until, one half-devil-half-witch waltzed into the Overworld uninvited and stole a precious artifact.

With a charming face and smooth talking words, the young devil-witch dazzled Fate. It had been so long since the last time she had actually conversed with another. The ideas of a visit from a being that could walk through the veils that kept humans from the Overworld and Underworld played on her heartstrings; played them like a master composer.

Their time together was brief. In his first visit she only learned his name: Drammelech; Elech as his family called him. She offered him her title in lieu of her name: Fate. He had flashed her a wide smile with the hint of a dimple at its corner and said that she must have known he'd come for her. She laughed off his flirty nature and relished the time they spoke.

He brought her a single fluffy pink flower on his next visit.

"What is this?"

"Rue."

"Rue? Why would you bring me something with such a sad connotation attached to its name?" Fate studied the young man before her.

"Because I rue that I cannot have you in my everyday life. Your beauty speaks to me in a way that nothing in my realm ever has." Bashful eyes lowered, punctuating his proclamation with the light stain of red that colored his cheeks.

It was in that one simple confession that her heart filled as it never had before. She took great pains to make sure every moment of their time together was well spent; full of laughter, conversation, and genuine happiness. On one particular visit, when Elech asked to see more than the main chamber of her Overworld post, she didn't hesitate before taking him into her most favorite room; the records room.

She led him into the vault where every being's scroll was kept under lock and key. It reminded her of the warehouses that her charges were so keen on using to store useless baubles and tokens. The difference was that this chamber was unending.

The day she had taken over for the previous soul, she had been shown into this very chamber of vastness that seemed larger than anything she could comprehend. She recalled asking in a hushed tone how big the chamber was. The look on her predecessor's face was enough of an answer that no more words had been needed.

In her years, she had tried to understand the organization of the vast room, but she had yet to figure out the magical system to the order of the scrolls. Although, the easiest to find belonged to the mystical beings which lived among the humans. Those scrolls always appeared near the front of the shelves and often had brightly colored symbols on the exterior of the rolled parchment.

With every falling grain of sand in the constantly flowing hourglass that mimicked the time of her charges, scrolls would appear or disappear as if they had always been as they were with the next drop. She oftentimes wondered if the disappearing scrolls reappeared elsewhere in the cavernous chamber, but to venture forth in search of them would take longer than she could spare. In the turn of her back, turmoil could erupt amongst her charges since time in the Overworld didn't work the same as it did on Earth. With that in mind, her forays into this chamber were typically the highlight of her time spent in the Overworld.

Fate stepped aside and allowed Elech into this sacred space. It gave her a sense of joy to be able to share this place with someone. The majestic nature of it all never failed to take her breath away and she wanted so much to see her joy reflected in his piercing eyes. She watched, rapt, as a wash of emotions rolled over his handsome face.

"What is this place?" Awe laced every word.

"I call it the chamber of records." She fingered the delicate shell of the hourglass. "This is where the universe balances. Within the scrolls, there is a tenuous balance struck between light, dark, old, new, beginnings, and endings."

Elech walked farther into the room and ran a hand along a row housing mounds of scrolls. His fingers settled on one and slipped it from the shelf. With gentle fingers, he unrolled the parchment and scanned it.

"What if this scroll were to get misplaced?" He rerolled the record and held it between his thumb and forefinger like it might burn him.

"It mustn't." Fate moved toward him and snatched the scroll from his grasp. "This single scroll represents the life of one of my charges and if something were to change, another scroll would surely appear to act as balance." She gently slid the scroll back into its place on the shelf.

Elech nodded and walked back to the main opening in the chamber. Beside the hourglass was a podium that held the largest tome the world never knew existed. Its leather wrapped spine was the glue that held all of Earth's existence together. Tucked into the pages of the book laid the blade of the most powerful item in the chamber: Fate's dagger. Her predecessor had gone to great lengths to reiterate the importance of keeping it hidden away, and now his words resurfaced in the forefront of her mind as Elech drew closer and closer to its resting place. An item of such power could be used to do so much damage in the world in the wrong hands, but in hers it was the instrument to set things gone awry on a corrected path. A sigh left her lips as Elech inspected the hourglass.

Fate watched the steady trickle of sand and moved to her left. She fingered the thick leather-bound tome that was home to a list of names and slid the jeweled silver hilt from between the book's pages. It felt heavy in her hand as she tucked it into the garter beneath her long flowing skirt. The knowledge that it was safe gave her a sense of peace.

Elech's next visit was years later even though the time passed in seemingly the blink of an eye. This time when he came to her, he appeared a full grown man even though she knew his age to still be young by her charges' standards. Instead of another pink fluffy rue, he held in his hand a long stemmed white rose.

"I thought you might've forgotten me," she remarked as she accepted his offering.

"Never."

His voice was deep, full-bodied, and sent a chill racing down her spine. When his hands slid down her arms, an actual shiver sliced through her body. How long had it been since she had felt the touch of another? Long before being assigned to her current post, that's for sure. She arched into him, pleased to find him hard and angular beneath her wanton fingers. In the space of a breath he had her in his arms, hands scorching over her exposed skin until fabric balled into his eager hands. His mouth, warm on her chaste lips, tasted like sunshine and a warm summer's breeze.

Fate threw caution and all her dignity into the wind and succumbed to Elech. With each tantalizing touch of his fingers against her flesh, she basked in the sensations of seduction. The anomaly of a fluttering in her chest that had earned her this post, kicked up as his tentative touches became more determined on their trail up her thighs beneath her skirt. She closed her eyes and cherished the intimacy of her predicament until a tug sent her eyes wide. The cool blade of the dagger she wore in the garter against her thigh sliced though her delicate flesh in a rush of warm, sticky liquid. Before she could defend herself, the press of the blade against her throat halted any further movement.

"I hate to do this," Elech whispered in her ear. "But you are the only thing standing between me and greatness." He pressed his lips to hers in a final kiss as the blade dug into her skin once more, this time slicing across her throat until it became hard to breathe. The fluttering in her chest that made her more human than ethereal catapulted, racing toward a finish line she could no longer sense. Elech stood, wiped the broad side of the blade against his trousers and blinked out of the realm.

Without her to dictate the course of human existence, chaos was sure to ensue, but protecting her charges from whatever evil Elech planned was more important. With her last breaths, she dragged herself into the chamber of records and sealed the doors behind her with all of her remaining magic. Now he would need more than just his smooth words to get into the chamber. Satisfied with her fortitude and forethought, she crumpled into a heap on the floor, knocking scrolls about on her way down. As much as she wanted to retrieve them and put them right again, she no longer had the strength. She stared at the scattered rolls of parchment, most decorated with symbols she knew instinctively. The mess on the floor would surely change the course of life for her beloved charges, but how, she could only guess.

Her last thought flashed through her brain on the fading embers of light in her soul. "What have I done?"

Available now for purchase where ebooks are sold.